THE TRAIL
WITHOUT END

**Center Point
Large Print**

**This Large Print Book carries the
Seal of Approval of N.A.V.H.**

ॐ श्री गणेशाय नमः

LAURAN PAINE

THE TRAIL WITHOUT END

CENTER POINT PUBLISHING
THORNDIKE, MAINE

This Center Point Large Print edition
is published in the year 2002 by arrangement with
Golden West Literary Agency.

The text of this Large Print edition is unabridged.
In other aspects, this book may vary from the original
edition. Printed in Thailand. Set in 16-point
Times New Roman type by Bill Coskrey.

ISBN 1-58547-099-6

Library of Congress Cataloging-in-Publication Data

Paine, Lauran.
   The trail without end / Lauran Paine.--Center Point large print ed.
      p. cm.
   ISBN 1-58547-099-6 (lib. bdg. : alk. paper)
      1. Montana--Fiction. 2. Large type books. I. Title.

PS3566.A34 T746 2002
813'.54--dc21

2001047470

LAURAN PAINE

THE TRAIL WITHOUT END

CENTER POINT PUBLISHING
THORNDIKE, MAINE

This Center Point Large Print edition
is published in the year 2002 by arrangement with
Golden West Literary Agency.

The text of this Large Print edition is unabridged.
In other aspects, this book may vary from the original
edition. Printed in Thailand. Set in 16-point
Times New Roman type by Bill Coskrey.

ISBN 1-58547-099-6

Library of Congress Cataloging-in-Publication Data

Paine, Lauran.
 The trail without end / Lauran Paine.--Center Point large print ed.
 p. cm.
 ISBN 1-58547-099-6 (lib. bdg. : alk. paper)
 1. Montana--Fiction. 2. Large type books. I. Title.

PS3566.A34 T746 2002
813'.54--dc21

2001047470

CONTENTS

ONE

THE LAND IN SPRINGTIME

The sun was easing down the high curve of speckled sky towards the west, changing colour as it went, which was how every summer day ended. But this was March and the time of day was slightly past four in the afternoon, and there were snowfields half down the sombre, massive mountains that shone like polished bone, so summer was still over the horizon even though the days had been a blessing for the past two weeks.

But every year it happened like this, and people had got to depend upon it. Sometime between the first of February and the end of March there were ten days to two weeks of perfect weather.

People were usually ready when it came. In all the towns storekeepers shoved winter goods to the rear and pulled summer goods to the fore. Freight and livery yards glowed with forge heat and rang to the music of anvils while barefooted stock was brought in to be shod and roached and curried to keep the slipping winter-hair shedding freely. Quagmire roadways hardened, sunshine bounced off an awakening earth, off sidehill snowbanks, off rooftops and mountaintops with a brilliance that made people squint.

Only the high country of mountains and snow-choked big valleys remained locked in with winter. But then, they were always the last to know summer and the first to witness its departure.

There were advantages both ways. Down across the immensity of the plainlands where it was warm and brilliant, and the sleeping earth was beginning to acquire a hint of pale green, the business of orderly social activity was starting to flourish again after the long restriction of winter. In the uplands, elk herds still pawed for roughage, squirrels still slept in a ball, and although the bears would be wakening soon, they had not stirred as yet, and on the thrusting promontory where the log-sod house stood facing outward and downward towards that flatter, warmer plainland, it was possible for a person to see the sunshine and activity down there, while at one's back were the rims and peaks and secret places, the valleys and benchlands and aspen-parks where winter remained undisturbed.

The house, having been created from its surroundings, blended so well that, especially with two feet of snow atop its broad roof, there was always a good possibility that it might escape detection from two-legged as well as four-legged critters.

That was no accident. When its builder had selected his wintering place that town down there at the upper end of the North Fork River did not exist. In those times it was like lying atop a cliff and spying; almost all movement originated down there on that huge plainland. Sometimes it had been possible to watch migrating redskin hordes coming back in springtime, straggle for three and four days from so far out over the junction of prairie and sky, they seemed no larger than fleas. Other times, it had been possible to watch buffalo darken a third of that entire grassland. The house was like a sentinel post, like a vigil-point of the *ozuye we tawatas,* the men of war. But for the Long Sleep, for the months when no sunshine appeared and grey daylight came late and departed early, it was also, like the treehole of the grey squirrel, a warm and pleasant place of hibernation. A man on snowshoes tending trap lines was as lonely, and as alone, as First Man. Sometimes he could almost see the face of God, and in a hush so deep it was without beginning or end, he could almost hear His word. Almost.

Between the town of North Fork, though, and that forest-sheltered log house there existed more than a distance of miles; there was a distance of time. Old Cade, who had built the cabin, used to say that all a man had to do to feel this difference was to face the prairie which was ever-changing to see the present, and maybe even get a glimpse of the future, then turn around and face the mountains, and see the past all the way back to the Beginning. It was true.

Cade also used to say that when a man began carrying a pocket-watch he put behind him everything having to

9

do with the real meaning of existence, and that was harder to understand, at least until Old Cade had been under his cairn six or eight years and the boy he'd found half dead from cold and had taken in, became a man with a solitary man's ways of thinking, then it made sense.

Old Cade had been a good teacher. He could not read nor write but he knew the meaning of every sign, man-made or natural, and he knew what was good from what was bad. He was a dead shot even in his last years, but never a hasty one. He never regretted the past, which was something else he taught the boy, because, as he said, if a man finds his needs and never exceeds them just for the sake of hoarding, why then he'll not be breaking any of the laws that govern life.

But life was not an easy experience; he taught the boy all the ways of survival, worked him hard, fed him well, encouraged the boy to laugh and walk straight and never lay a hand to anything that did not belong to him.

Just before Old Cade died—and he knew to the day when that time was to be—he sat in late-day warmth outside on the porch that extended east and west the full length of the log house, and told him it was the most natural thing on earth for the strong, when they felt the urge, to go rutting. A man's neck didn't swell like that of a bull elk, and he had no horns to sharpen by honing them against treetrunks, but it was the same nevertheless when the springtime urges came.

So, he had said to the boy, the time would shortly arrive when the boy would close the cabin, saddle up, take his guns and ride down to the prairie, and although the boy would consider himself motivated by curiosity, it would be something in him that went a lot deeper. What a man should remember above all other things, was that he was a man; not a skulking wolf, not a disagreeable bear, not a timid tree-squirrel, and not a stupid buffalo bull. He was a man, the equal of any other man, and he owed respect to the ways of others, but most of all he owed it to himself.

Cade had died, the boy had planted him in the place where Cade had been carrying up boulders for his cairn for thirty years, then the boy closed the cabin that March, and did exactly as Cade had known he would do. He had saddled up, cast a final look backwards, then, with the rifle cradled in one arm, he had reined the horse down towards the golden-lighted Montana prairielands, and in every way that mattered, the boy was a man.

North Fork saw them all come and go. It had started out as an outpost with a soldier-fort athwart the ancient redskin road leading from the lower country to the high country. There had to be trouble about that of course; settlers always planted their towns where there was a river, timber, good graze, and hopefully, mild winters.

Those same things were essential to the Sioux and Blackfeet, and although they had never owned a village where North Fork came to be, their war and hunting trail went squarely through the area where those first bearded argonauts erected their town. It took a long time and a lot of bitterness to get the army up there. By the time its first thin column appeared, the settlers had pretty well established their sovereignty, but they—and the Indians—had paid dearly.

A lot of people resented the army's arrogance, its authoritarian methods, when, by the time it started snaking down the logs for its fort, settlers had already taught the redskins to stay well clear of North Fork. Unless, of course, they just plain wanted to fight.

Some of those people were still around but the army had abandoned its outpost fifteen years back. There had been no trouble with Indians for six or eight years prior to that time, although, if a person really wanted to, he could poke around in the upland meadows, the plateaux cut off on all sides by miles of forests of immense pines and fir trees, and find an occasional little band of break-outs, Indians who were fugitives because they had fled the reservations in an attempt to recapture a way of life that was no more and never would be again.

But no one bothered. Times had changed and were changing still. Those people from a half century back, red or white, owned a backwash that no one else cared a damn about.

The buffalo were also gone, replaced by cattle, and the proud lance-bearers in war-bonnets had their places taken by rangeriders on better horses, but whose code was no different, really, except that North Fork had law nowadays and such things as individual combat, raids by neighbours upon neighbours, daring and clever thefts, and long, aimless meanderings in search of game, or simply death, were not tolerated if they were any kind of a threat to social living and the common security.

Not very much remained of Uncle Sam's log fort up closer to the foothills now. People had been helping themselves for years, to the walls and roofs, but mostly to the doors and windows and hardware; those things were not just rare, they were also prohibitively expensive since they had to come to North Fork in freight wagons, sometimes from as far southward as Denver.

But the town, older than the fort, had all its major structures by that warm, bland March. It even had stone mounting blocks out front of some of the stores, a sure sign of substance and sophistication on the frontier where every place of business had hitchracks, but very few had elegant big square stones for folks, mostly ladies, to use in mounting their horses or in stepping daintily into their buggies.

North Fork had a huge, cavernous general store, called the *Emporium*. It had a Presbyterian church in mid-town, and it had a stage company way-station at the south end, with a palisaded wagon-yard, and an even bigger freight yard at the north end of town, near the road that crossed the mountains.

There was a gunsmith's shop, a saddle and harness

works, three saloons and even a combination dress shop and bakery, which was across the main thoroughfare, called Lincoln Street, from the log jailhouse, which stood to one side of the combination firehall and local justice court. Above this civic building there was a cupola made of planed lumber that housed the firebell, and between episodes of real trouble, the town marshal, a greying, shaggy man named Johnathon Barlow, was harassed by young boys with slingshots whose delight was to fire rocks at the bell to make it ring, after which they fled in breathless excitement and watched people come running, because the only time the bell was supposed to be rung was when some disaster threatened the community.

The clear echo of that bell had been heard by Old Cade and the boy a number of times, over the years, when they had hunted or trapped at the lower elevations, down near the big prairie. It had a tone that carried for miles and miles, and because the air was always glass-clear, and in wintertime was also thin with cold, almost any sound that was at all loud, came up and bounced back and forth through the foremost mountains.

North Fork also had trees, something else that was not common in frontier towns. It had three public troughs between the north and south ends of town, and it had a number of fraternal organizations including the Ladies' Altar Society, a Masonic affiliation, and a lodge of The Exalted And Mystic Brotherhood Of The Golden

Circle, which was known locally as the brotherhood of bar-room bums and saddletramps.

TWO

AMONG THE HIVE-DWELLERS

The most critical people in life seemed to be the ones most open to criticism themselves.

As far as Dick Ullman was concerned, no one was sharper, shrewder or smarter than he was, particularly when it came to horseflesh, and there was some truth in that, but being a lifelong horsetrader and liveryman did not necessarily carry with it any guarantees beyond those endemic in horsetrading.

Dick was a large, thick, powerful man, slow on his feet, like a bear, and with the same small malevolent tawny eyes. He was in his forties and had been a livestock dealer since his early teens. He had also been a lot of other things, most of which were in one way or another connected with livestock, but for the last thirteen years he had owned and operated the North Fork Trading & Livery Barn, a large, long, building with pole corrals out back and sheds adjacent to the back alley which housed a shoeing shop, a granary and a catch-all storage facility.

Dick was scarred and respected, the results of an unpredictable temperament, but he had a virtue, he was good to animals. It was people he had to challenge, had to prove himself against. He had two hostlers, a dayman and a nightman, both wispy, older men, who lived in fear of his anger and his big fists. When Dick sneered at someone riding in to stable a horse, the hostlers took their cue from that and also sneered. Dick was one of those men whose personality was so overpowering that weaker men, without genuine personalities of their own, borrowed his and if they were around him long enough, became pale shadows in their likenesses.

People usually tolerated Dick Ullman; a few liked him, but most people conducted whatever business they had with Ullman and let it go at that.

Town Marshal Johnathon Barlow, as tall a man as Ullman but not as thick nor corded, had once said that every place he had ever been there had always been at least one Dick Ullman, and like a work-horse, they were useful but a person was not obliged to invite them to supper.

Marshal Barlow made that statement the day following the big battle in Mike Clancy's saloon, the Montana House, when Dick had taken on too big a load, which was unusual because although Dick drank he rarely ever did so to excess, and dredged up an ancient disagreement with John Barlow which resulted in Barlow calling Dick a liar, and the fists flew.

It was a matter of prejudice who emerged victor. Most people liked John Barlow and did not much care for

Dick Ullman, so it was said John had won, but Barlow had been in the sawdust four times to Ullman's twice, and for two days afterwards Barlow ached all over as though he'd been sick with a fever, while Dick's black eye, split mouth, and torn and swollen right ear were all external, and otherwise he seemed little the worse for his battle.

But that had happened years back. Since then Dick and Marshal Barlow had got along famously. Ullman was a man who had respect only for those people he knew, from personal experience, deserved it.

Dick despised redskins next to thieves and liars, and next in order were the men who rode in, not very often any more, carrying long-barrelled rifles cradled in their arms, and who looked, dressed, acted, and sometimes smelled, as gamey as squaw-men. He had a reason. There was a raw red scar across Ullman's chest, a memento of a meeting with one of those back-country whiteskins when, in his early youth, Ullman had been taken as a slave to live with a band of renegade redskins, led by a huge, red-bearded whiteman, after the renegades had butchered Ullman's parents and sisters on the flats across the Missouri River, in Omaha country. The knife-scar came when that red-bearded renegade had caught Ullman trying to escape; if the renegade had not been drunk that night he would have killed young Ullman. As it was, Ullman lay for a month more dead than alive.

The red-bearded whiteskin should have finished the job. His neglect cost him his life two years later when Dick Ullman stood six feet in his moccasins and weighed well over two hundred pounds.

One of the mistakes people make is in believing young men never forget and older men do; it works the other way around. When the tall, sinewy young man rode up as shaggy-headed as a bear with that rifle cradled across his arm, the pistol belted to his middle under the worn blanket-coat, and dismounted making the toed-in sign of moccasin marks in the soft earth out front, everything Dick Ullman had never forgot came quickly, and hotly, to life, even though he had not seen a man like that in some years. Certainly not a *young* one. Mountain Men had been dying out for half a century; their time, like that of the buffalo hunters, was well past.

Ullman strode forth from inside his barn two yards behind his dayman, who was accepting the reins from the stranger, and without a word wrenched the reins away and thrust them back.

'Go somewhere else,' he growled deep down, pushing the reins forward. 'I don't take in horses belonging to your kind. Probably a stolen horse anyway. Take 'em!' He thrust his rein-fist against the younger man's middle. 'Take 'em and git!'

The hostler faded back. The younger man showed nothing, neither astonishment, which he was entitled to feel, nor anger. He took the reins without a word, studied

Dick Ullman over a moment of roiled silence, then led his horse on up the road.

Dick spat and swore, and called out. 'Hey, you stinkin' renegade, before I change my mind and break your back, you light out of North Fork back to your cave!'

The youth kept on walking. He had been here before, but years back with Cade. That time, too, he had felt something; not just that these people were different, but something like a deeper current. He had never asked and Old Cade had never explained, beyond making a comment as they led their pack animals back towards the mountains.

'It's the same with people whether you pack 'em in together against their will on a reservation, or whether they herd together in a town out of choice—they come to hate any kind of free man, any kind of natural man.'

That was it.

There was no other public barn in North Fork, but up at the north end of town, beyond the freight yard, there was a public corral. That was where the young man left his horse and went in search of feed, which he bought from a freighter, a rough but tolerant man who also said the young man could leave his saddle, bridle, rifle and blanket-roll in the man's wagon, if he wished. Otherwise, someone was sure to steal them, worthless though they were.

The youth afterwards padded soundlessly down to the

Emporium and entered, then stood transfixed by the array of wonders which included everything from Winchester saddleguns to bolt goods, ladies' dresses direct from St Louis, French toilet water all the way from Chicago, and a genuine glass case full of watches and rings and necklaces that sparkled in the late-day sunlight.

This was the store from which he had carried out supplies to Old Cade years back, and had afterwards helped the old man lash the packs to their extra horses. He had never forgot it. Sometimes, on long nights, he had lain awake in his bunk remembering, and, when he had been much younger, he had figured out that heaven probably was just like the interior of the *Emporium*.

A thick-set man with jet-black eyes wearing paper sleeve-guards, saw him and studied him, then strolled over. There was another man with paper cuffs, a clerk, and there were six or eight customers too, who saw the young man, and regarded him with different kinds of interest.

The black-eyed man owned the store. His name was Alexander Farraday. He was a man of influence in the North Fork country, a widower with a girl named Angeline. He was also a man whose memory was good enough to know who the tall young man was although he had not seen him in several years.

'Thought you'd left the country,' he said, being amiable even though he could feel the hostility behind him in the customers, some of them anyway, and also in his clerk. 'Douglas Weldon, isn't it?'

The young man smiled. 'Douglas Cade Weldon.'

The black-eyed man's gaze mellowed. 'Yes. Every now and then I think back.' As though at a loss for the correct words, which in fact he really was, the black-eyed man wagged his head. 'Well; what can I do for you this afternoon?'

Young Weldon kept his smile. 'Nothing, I reckon, Mister Farraday. I just wanted to stand here and look around again.'

Farraday was a businessman but he was also a father, and although he did not really understand this young man, he understood how it must have been with him, up there atop Old Cade's mountain living like a hermit, or a stealthy damned redskin. 'You look all you like,' he said, 'and if you see something you like, let me know.'

Farraday made up for Ullman.

The first day passed quickly, but then the young man had not reached town until afternoon. Dusk came early, for even though it felt like summer it was still early springtime, the storefronts were eventually dark and the plank-walks echoed to only an occasional footfall. Lamplight glowed from the houses out back of the main roadway, and this, for some reason, was always a time of melancholy for Douglas Cade Weldon. Since Old Cade had left, this was the time of day when memory, and something else, something that existed loosely inside him and which he had never been able to hold down and describe, or give a name to, haunted him.

Only now that he was in the town, the feelings were worse. On the mountain, sunset had meant it was time to head for the cabin. Down here, oncoming dusk meant that everyone else headed for home and Douglas Cade Weldon lingered behind.

He went to Clancy's bar. Old Cade kept a cache of jug-whiskey so the young man was no novice to the stuff, but Old Cade had set a limit for them both and neither exceeded it himself nor allowed the young man to exceed it, but at Clancy's bar a man not only could drink as much as he wished to, they encouraged him to drink that much, and as much more as he could get down.

Suppertime was a dull hour for Clancy's place. Later, things would liven up, especially on the week-end nights, but for a while as Douglas Cade Weldon leaned and sipped smooth sourmash whiskey and smiled at old Clancy's tall tales of the earlier times when he remembered Old Cade as half-man, half-grizzly, there was hardly a sound in the entire big saloon. It was almost as quiet inside as it was outside.

Three rangeriders were down the bar humped over and standing one-legged like sandhill cranes, drinking and talking, now and then laughing, minding their own business, booted and spurred, and armed, heeding neither Clancy nor the whipcord young man in the blanket-coat and moccasins at the other end of the bar.

Otherwise, there were two rickety ancients at a battered table near the iron stove playing pinochle. Between them on the floor was a box of dirt. Each of them spat amber from time to time into this box.

Mike Clancy was a blue-eyed beer-barrel of a man with a wild thatch that always, even on Sunday when Clancy wore his celluloid collar and a genuine necktie in honour of the Sabbath, looked as though it had just been combed with a barn rake.

Clancy was a lot older than he looked. He was also a lot less congenial, when the time came, than his perpetual affability indicated that he was.

Clancy knew a lot about growing up wild, and although his way had been entirely different from the way of Old Cade's boy, there were things Clancy understood that only another orphan grown to manhood could understand.

When the boy, after his second drink, spoke out, Clancy listened leaning on his bar, and said, 'You just remember, Young Cade, there's got to be all kinds. Ullman is a disagreeable man to be sure, and he's got reasons, but once you cut off the shag and throw away thim moccasins, and commence wearing boots, and shirts with buttons on 'em, and all, Ullman'll niver notice you.'

It seemed like good advice. Young Weldon had his third drink on it and by then a few other patrons were beginning to drift in.

A man could never truly be like other men, the tall trapper from Cade Mountain knew that, just by instinct, because he also knew no two men looked alike, talked alike, or reacted alike, but a man could dress like other men, and could come in time to even behave the same way, which was what Clancy had been trying to convey to him.

Douglas Cade Weldon was willing. Now that he had come down to the prairielands to mingle and be among other people, he was perfectly willing to be as like them as he could.

He had his third drink, then had no more even though he lingered in the saloon because it was warm and redolent and pleasant there, where the loneliness could not reach, and decided that the next morning he would buy the things at Farraday's store that would make him just about indistinguishable from these people he now intended to stay among.

THREE

DEATH IS NO STRANGER

The nights cooled off quickly, and would continue to do so for another two months, at the very least, but men whose physical exertions during the warm and pleasant days conditioned them for the labouring of the summer to come, opened the new season almost every night, now, by arriving at the Montana House on foot from town, in wagons from the outskirts, or on horseback from the distant ranches.

Clancy's saloon was not only the most popular bar in town—there were two others—it also had the reputation of being the most decorous, although that was not really an appellation that had been coined with *any* saloon in mind.

By eight o'clock the bar was crowded, there were poker and fan-tan and twenty-one games in progress at the wall-tables, and newcomers, rangeriders recently arrived after wintering in the warmer southlands, in search of work now that the cow-camp season was shortly to begin again, whooped and howled when they were able to renew old acquaintances.

Douglas Cade Weldon had never seen anything like it. He found a chair in an out-of-the-way corner and observed it all, scarcely noticed by the surging, noisy crowd of customers, although those three cowboys who had been in the saloon earlier, from time to time, between drinks, looked down his way and talked among themselves with grins, and pointedly commented. They were not old enough to have the kind of bitter memories that provoked the resentment of men like Dick Ullman, but they had heard enough of the old stories. Still, they were not vicious men, just fun-loving; they were rangemen, and among that fellowship there was nothing more delightful than a practical joke. If it resulted in someone's chagrin, or perhaps even a little physical pain, so much the better.

By nine o'clock they had perfected their plan. One of them ambled down where young Weldon sat, appeared through purest accident to hook a spur beneath the rung of Weldon's chair, and dumped both chair and man backwards into the sawdust on the floor. The cowboys laughed as Weldon struggled around to regain his feet and to pick up the chair. Other men also laughed, but they only saw someone fall awkwardly and did not know it had been no accidental tumble.

It was cow-camp humour. Not really funny at all, but to men who needed a release, not just for the nettlesomeness inspired by a long, dreary afternoon of drinking and boredom, but also as an outlet for the kind of neglect cowboys usually found awaiting them in towns where they were not usually viewed with much sympathy or favour, it was an excuse to laugh, to achieve some notice, and maybe it was also a way of showing that there were men even lower on the social scale than they were; someone they could scorn the way townspeople usually scorned cowboys.

One man had seen it all because he had been sensing the mood of those three all evening: Mike Clancy. No one had to condone a bar-keeper's vocation—which the Ladies' Altar Society of North Fork most certainly did not—but there was something worth noting about long-time saloon-men; they could sense moods and temperaments quicker and better among all the varying kinds of men who frequented their establishments, than the best mind-readers on earth.

Clancy went unobtrusively down the bar where Marshal Barlow was nursing a nickel beer and said, 'Keep an eye on those three, John, they're primed for trouble.'

That was all that came of the practical joke, right then. Douglas Cade Weldon brushed off the sawdust and accepted the drawled apology of the cowboy who had upset him, and re-set his chair red to the ears, but smiling. He thought it had been an accident.

Twenty minutes later, though, when another of the cowboys took his turn at what was called 'chousing', heading down the bar with a too-full beer glass, Clancy gave Barlow the nod, and the town marshal moved. He caught up with the cowboy, touched his shoulder, and when the cowboy turned Barlow said, 'That's enough. Drink it, don't spill it on him.'

The cowboy stared, then he stiffened. Other men who were near enough to comprehend, grinned at the joke that had backfired, and that humiliated the rangerider. He reached carefully to set the glass atop the bar, then he turned fully and said, 'What the hell you talking about, Marshal? A man's got a right to drink in here, ain't he?'

Barlow was finished with it, as far as he was concerned. 'Sure. Drink all you want. Just leave the stranger alone.'

The other two riders sauntered closer to hear. One of

them, a shockle-headed red-faced man had to have his say. 'You're starting out chousing riders kind of early, aren't you, Marshal?'

Johnathon Barlow, like Mike Clancy, knew what he was coming up against, now, and still sought to avoid it as he started past towards the bar. 'Forget it. Leave it lie. Just don't go trouble-hunting in here tonight.'

The red-faced man took that up at once. 'Why gawd-damn you,' he called, loudly enough to be heard all over the room, his words bringing on a pall of quick silence. 'You got no call to throw your weight around when no one's making trouble.'

Marshal Barlow faced back and studied those three. Clancy had been dead right. Barlow tried one last time to pass it off. 'I said leave it be.'

Clancy also tried to pass it off. 'Hey, you boys, one drink on the house. Come get it.'

The humiliated cowboy, flushed in the face, his eyes liquid-shiny, moved clear of the bar to face Barlow. He was the one needing satisfaction, not his red-faced friend. 'You ain't going to open season on us, you bas-tard,' he called to Barlow, and went for his hip-holster.

Men bumped hard against one another trying to get clear. Someone dropped a bottle that broke into a thou-sand fragments against the brass boot-rail. Mike Clancy dived under the bar for his shotgun, and John Barlow whipped sideways as he went for his Colt. The cowboy fired first, turning Barlow still more to one side as his bullet struck high into meat and bone. Barlow's gun was out but exploded into the floor as impact hurled him against the bar.

From far back the man in the old blanket-coat called ahead. 'Your turn, cowboy!'

But the rider who had fired was concentrating on Barlow and probably did not even hear Weldon. His red-faced friend did though. He was already facing in the right direction. He dropped low and streaked for his gun. Weldon fired from the right side and the red-faced cowboy went down looking completely surprised. That made the other one spin, his cocked Colt homing in with a blur of speed. Weldon fired again, the same way. To a man who had been living with guns atop Cade's mountain all his maturing years, this kind of shooting was purest murder. The second cowboy went backwards and his muzzleblast was aimed at the ceiling.

The third rider was like stone, suddenly as sober as a man could be. He looked ponderously from his two dead friends to the ancient, long-barrelled revolver in the hand of the lanky man in the old blanket-coat.

Mike Clancy pushed his shotgun into this one's back, up near the shoulderblades and ordered him to throw his gun on the floor. The cowboy was too stunned to obey, so a bearded freighter reached and disarmed the cowboy for Clancy.

The crowd surged up and hid Marshal Barlow from sight. North Fork did not have a surgeon or even a physician, but Dick Ullman, who had been doctoring on horses and other animals all his life, was sent for, and when Barlow lost consciousness four men carried him across and made him as comfortable as they could on a bunk in one of his cells. Over there, Ullman could do a better job anyway, gouging out the slug that had shattered Barlow's left arm up close to the shoulder, and had then exited at the upper joint making a great, jagged hole. Barlow was very lucky; a forty-four lead slug fired at a man from a distance not exceeding fifteen feet ordinarily minced the meat and bone and muscle beyond repair. Later, men said the only thing that saved the marshal was his quick twist sideways. Otherwise, he'd have caught that lead in the brisket and would have been killed on the spot.

They also had something else to say: Not many had seen young Weldon draw, and only a few more than that had seen him fire the first time, but almost everyone had been looking when he'd fired the last shot, and what seemed to Douglas Cade Weldon to be sheer murder, had seemed to those less experienced armsmen as an almost uncannily unbelievable marksmanship. Both those dead cowboys had been killed by bullets that hit them dead centre in the middle of the breastbone—right through their hearts.

Dick Ullman called it a freak bit of luck, but Mike Clancy, who had been there when Ullman hadn't, said it was no such thing. 'That feller knew exactly where thim bullets was going, and if anyone can get him to do it again, I'll lay money that he can do it every time he tries to. And I'll tell you something else: maybe the rest of the town don't like a man in moccasins and with hair long enough to braid, and maybe Dick hates his kind, but if I was Ullman and the rest of North Fork, I wouldn't push young Cade too hard. I knew the old man as raised him. Old Cade taught the lad well, you can believe that, and Old Cade was a man the redskins used to make up songs about.'

It was a bad night, and the next day it was no better. Douglas Cade Weldon was not concerned with the two rangemen; they had deserved exactly what they had got. He had killed rank boar-bears that had charged, trying to kill him, and he had killed panthers, too, that had stalked him. He knew exactly what a man had to do, at times like those. As Clancy had said, Old Cade had taught him well.

But that night, when he went over and watched Ullman work with blood to his wrists, saving the town marshal's life, he regretted very much coming down off his mountain. The last thing he had wanted was the kind of notoriety he was now getting.

The next day it was even worse because by then the story had begun to gather embellishments. When he went down to the *Emporium* to buy the boots and shirt and trousers, and the socks too, and the stiff-brimmed rangeman's hat, although Alex Farraday did not mention the fight—did not in fact even seem to want to talk to young Weldon at all, even though he personally waited on him—everyone who was in the store stopped what they were doing and stared. Outside, it was the same, except that an occasional man smiled and called a kind of greeting—usually calling him Young Cade because they did not know his name, and that was what Clancy called him—or, as at the café where he went to eat, well-meaning men told him they approved of what he had done, that those damned lousy troublesome rangeriders needed to be put in their places.

Only two men, one the freighter who had allowed young Weldon to store his saddle and gun in the wagon, and a man he had never seen before, the gunsmith whose shop was on the west side of the main thoroughfare, offered him advice. The freighter said, 'Son, don't stay around here any longer'n you got to. Them two dead men have got friends and relatives somewhere, and they'll be looking you up.' The gunsmith, old and grizzled, but as keen-eyed as a foraging eagle, said, 'You trade off that oldtime dragoon pistol, boy, and you get a good, stiff, back-leather holster that's been waxed inside. You're going to need them both if you keep on doing things like you done in Clancy's place. Rightly, boy, that warn't none of your business.'

'They'd have killed him,' said Weldon. 'And all he was trying to do was make them settle down. He didn't have a chance at three to one.'

The old gunsmith just smiled and nodded. 'I know, boy, I know. Every place I ever been's got a graveyard full of heroes. Even right here in North Fork. Well; tell you what I'll do—just for old times' sake because I knew Old Cade fifty years ago when he and I was still rutting—I'm going to buy his old pistol off'n you, then for the same money I'm going to sell you a forty-five Colt, with a six-inch barrel, and I'm going to throw in the holster. Boy, if there's one thing I never liked it was to see fellers your age, and knowing no more'n you know about places like North Fork—and all the rest of this lousy modern world—get ploughed under.'

Douglas did not trade. Old Cade's horse-pistol was out-dated ten years before its owner had died, but it was something solid in a man's hand, solid and weighty and honest, and it was just about all that was left to remind Douglas Weldon of the man who had left it for him, along with the ancient long-barrelled rifle with the birds-eye maple stock.

But he bought for hard cash the later-model gun and the fast-draw holster. Then he rode back into the foothills north of town to see how those two guns compared. The forty-five was a better gun, but young Weldon would not admit that for a long while because it seemed somehow to be a betrayal.

He had taken the gunsmith's advice, but he did not take the freighter's advice. In fact, he never saw the freighter again.

FOUR

KINDS OF MEN

Farraday was against it and so was Ullman, but for different reasons. Farraday said it was unfair to put young Weldon into that position; it might even be permanently damaging to him. Dick Ullman's objection was anchored in his darker depths.

'You let one of his kind have the gun-run of this town and I can tell you, because by gawd I know for a fact, you'll regret the day you ever so much as saw him. His kind's got no more compunction about killing a man than we have a blue-tailed fly.'

Gabe Longstreet who managed the stage company's way-station in North Fork, and who was serving a term as President of the Town Council, threw up his hands. Gabriel Longstreet was a very practical businessman with civic pride. He was younger than Alex Farraday or Dick Ullman, and he was not touched by things that seemed important to them. 'Then give me an alternative,' he exclaimed in frank exasperation. 'You know damned well the riding season's about here. We'll have cowboys shooting out the lamps again, and starting brawls in the middle of the road. You name me one man who'll have the job, instead of Weldon, and by gawd I'll vote to hire him right now, tonight. Name me one other man.'

It was the stormiest meeting of the North Fork Town Council in a long time. Normally, at least in wintertime when people did not have much else in the way of nightly entertainment, the council chamber, which was also the judicial district's courtroom in the fire-house, by day, would have had at least fifty spectators on the benches outside the railing, but tonight there was not a soul out there, and that made it possible for the councilmen to speak out.

Voting for someone to replace Marshal Barlow was unpleasant at its best. Not just because Barlow was a good lawman, but also because he was the friend of each councilman. But friendship was not going to change anything; Johnathon Barlow was out of it, as Gabe Longstreet had pointed out as soon as the meeting had been officially opened. He would not be able to even leave his bed for perhaps a month, and although it had been his left arm which had been injured, not his right one, and even if he could be up and around sooner, there was still the matter of law enforcement during the interim.

'He probably won't take the job anyway,' Farraday said. 'We're arguing about something we ought to have verified, first.'

'Well, *someone's* got to take it,' exclaimed Longstreet. 'Who else can you think of?'

Ullman had come to the meeting with an idea. 'We got about a month before the working season opens,' he told the others. 'That's enough time to write to some of the big cities and maybe hire a lawman that way.'

Longstreet said, 'Month hell, Dick. What happened the other night could happen again next week. Sure, the weather may turn bad again for a few weeks, but rangeriders are going to start drifting in just like those three did, from now on, and even if they weren't, we still got to have some law in town.'

Ullman, a man who never liked having his ideas shown as faulty, scowled. 'If you mean, hire a man right now, tomorrow or the next day, Gabe, we're right back where we started. There ain't one.'

Longstreet said, 'Weldon,' and Alex Farraday gave his head a weary shake. 'I'm against it.'

Ullman flared up. 'Why, Alex? Listen; there's no one else around. I'm against it too, Lord knows. But maybe Gabe's right, maybe we *got* to. But I'll tell you one thing, it's a damned poor choice. I know his kind.'

It was Ullman's about-face that clinched it. In any voting plurality of three it only took two votes to pass a proposition. Longstreet did not waste time. He made the proposal in the form of a legal motion, he and Ullman voted for it, and Alex Farraday threw up his hands. His parting words were: 'All right. You'd better talk to him, Gabe. Not you, Dick.'

That suited Ullman, and after tending to a few more trivial matters, the meeting broke up, someone blew down the lamp mantle to douse the light, and everyone went home.

Douglas Cade Weldon was sleeping soundly at the hotel that night, his new clothes and gun draped from a ladderback chair in the room he had upstairs that over-looked North Fork's main thoroughfare, as well as looked out beyond the stove pipes and rooftops to the mountains. He had no idea what had been discussed at the council meeting, not even the next morning when, after breakfast, he went down to the jailhouse to sit with Johnathon Barlow.

It did not seem right, some folks said, for Marshal Barlow to lie in the jailhouse. He had a room at the hotel. It was Barlow's idea that he stay where he was. He said it made it handier for Ullman to walk up from his trading barn to tend him, but what was really in the back of his mind was that by being in the jailhouse he could still keep his hand in, at law enforcement. Also, a lot of friends who would have hesitated to barge in and visit, upstairs at the hotel, had no such inhibitions about vis-iting him—or anyone else—over at the jailhouse.

In fact, when Douglas Cade Weldon entered, the man-ager of the local stage company was sitting on a stool in the cell talking very earnestly with Marshal Barlow. Both men looked up when Weldon walked in, and through the ensuing silence, both men stared intently. Weldon smiled at Barlow, and nodded perfunctorily at Longstreet, whom he knew only by sight.

The marshal was as weak as a kitten, as pale and

washed-out looking as a corpse, but his mind worked as well as ever except that he got sleepy if he talked and thought for very long. He greeted young Weldon, then introduced him to Gabriel Longstreet. He nodded towards another stool nearby and invited Weldon to sit a spell. Then Marshal Barlow went silent, and looked steadily at Gabe, whose duty it evidently was, to bring up the matter he and Barlow had been discussing before Douglas Cade Weldon had walked in.

Longstreet had misgivings the moment he looked into the clear, steady eyes of the younger man. Young Weldon did not always show much expression. He sat now, gazing at Longstreet with the calm impassivity of an Indian. He had a strong face, an untroubled one. He sat patiently waiting, and Longstreet was a little unnerved by his great depth of calm.

Johnathon Barlow sighed. 'The town council wants you to take over my job until I can be back on my feet, Douglas. Maybe that'll be a month or two.'

Young Weldon looked from Longstreet to Barlow, and shook his head. 'No thanks.' He stood up. 'I'll come around later, Marshal, about suppertime maybe.' He turned and walked out.

Gabe Longstreet stared after Weldon, then turned with a peculiar expression and said, 'Just like that? Maybe Ullman's right, John, maybe he *is* different.'

Barlow considered the fly-specked ceiling a moment. 'He's different. He's different in a way I wish to hell a lot more of us were. He was raised to say it straight out, whatever it was, and to be sure he was right.' Barlow moved his head on the blanket-roll pillow and searched Longstreet's face. 'For your sake, Gabe, I'm sorry he turned it down, but for his sake I'm glad he did. Listen; that boy's been raised up there in the mountains never to aim a gun without pulling the trigger, and never to lie nor steal nor make a promise he couldn't keep. I don't know how old he is, maybe twenty-three, twenty-four, but we got kids here in town of eight and ten who know more about towns and townfolks than Douglas Weldon does. He's got to have a year or two to learn all those things. Shoving a gun in his hand and sticking my badge on his shirt would be like—well—I don't know exactly what, but I'm glad he turned you down.'

That had been a long speech for Marshal Weldon. He afterwards settled flatly and closed his eyes. Gabe Longstreet departed, went down to Ullman's barn, first, with the news, then trudged over to the *Emporium* and caught Alex Farraday in his cluttered back-room office having a cup of coffee, and also told him.

Farraday pointed to the coffeepot on the woodstove as he said, 'Cup on the shelf above my desk, Gabe, help yourself . . . I'm glad.'

Longstreet helped himself to a cup and said, 'All right, you are glad. Where does that leave us, Alex?'

Farraday smiled benignly. 'Gabe, you seem to figure there's an army of cowboys headed this way primed to shoot up the town. Don't be so upset. We'll find someone, sooner or later.'

Longstreet stared. 'Damn it, Alex, last night at the meeting it was *you,* not me or Dick, who was sweating because we didn't have no law in town . . . Well; I was too, I reckon; but it was you—'

'That was last night,' Farraday interrupted to say. 'Things always seem clearer to me when I sleep on them. Maybe if we talked to Mike he would have some suggestions.'

Longstreet tasted the coffee, evidently found it satisfactory, and drank half the cupful before speaking again. 'Mike knows a lot of 'em, and nine-tenths are men I wouldn't hire to dung out a barn for me, let alone walk around town with a badge and a tied-down gun.'

'We can ask,' Farraday said, persevering, and smiled at his visitor. 'Mike's a good judge of men. He'll know the kind of man we need.'

Longstreet finished his coffee and turned, looking for a place to leave the cup as he said, 'Hell; everyone knows the kind of man we *need.* What no one seems to know is where we're going to find him.'

Longstreet left the general store, crossed to the west side of the road and turned to his right walking towards the way-station office and wagon-yard. As he passed the dingy gunsmith shop he glanced in. Young Weldon was in there, leaning on a workbench while old Stuart Campbell worked, the pair of them talking quietly. Gabe looked swiftly away and kept on walking.

The gunsmith had seen him. Very few people passed on either side of the road that old Stuart Campbell did not see. He had a mind like a steel trap; whatever he saw, he latched to, hard, and whatever he knew, he sifted and sorted until he could work it into a pattern that fit people. It was not just for the light that the gunsmith had his workbench facing the roadway window.

He grinned thinly as Longstreet strode past. 'He don't look too happy. Maybe you was the only man they wanted, to take Johnathon's place.'

Young Weldon glanced out but Longstreet's stride had already carried him from sight. But he knew, so he said, 'How many men are in North Fork?'

Old Campbell guessed the purpose of the question and shook his head. 'That ain't it, son. How many men in North Fork got the gumption for the job. *That's* the question. I'd say maybe a handful. Only, their wives and mammies and all would raise a ruckus if they took it.' Old Stuart grinned broadly. 'That leaves you and me; we don't have no family. I'm too old, and wouldn't touch the job if I wasn't, and you—well—you just been saying you got nothing against killing when it's forced on a man, but you figure it's wrong to make it your business to go round and chouse folks because they're making trouble for others.'

Old Campbell lifted the handgun he'd been working on, had been converting from .44 calibre to .45. He made a face. The gun in his hand was as heavy as a hammer, drooped at the barrel-end, and although functional enough, was a mass-produced weapon that had never felt the magic of a professional re-builder's genius.

'Feller'd be better off to hold this thing by the barrel and drive nails with it,' he said, disparagement making even his leathery old seamed face show the disgust that dripped from each word. 'What's this country coming to, arming men with things like this?' He put the gun aside and turned. 'You been practising?'

Young Weldon smiled. 'Just that one day, when I bought the gun new.'

Stuart Campbell gazed long at his visitor. 'Work all right, did it?'

'Yes. I never heard of waxing a holster before. Seems sort of dishonest, making a gun to come out that easy.'

The old gunsmith groaned. 'Boy, there quit being any honour in this damned world forty, fifty years ago. The way things are nowadays you don't das't take a man's word and turn your back or he'll shoot you between the shoulder blades. Nothing dishonest at all about being able to stay alive, as long as you're facing them when you fire. And you'd better ride up there now and then and keep practising, because it ain't the same at all, down here, as it was up there. A bear'll growl and a cat'll scream, but a two-legged catamount'll smile in your face and shoot you in the belly. You remember that.'

FIVE

ACTIONS AND REACTIONS

Douglas Cade Weldon rode north; without realizing it he turned to the mountains when he had troubled thoughts, or mind-asked questions. Practising with the gun was an excuse, not a reason. He had handled weapons since early boyhood, since his first autumn on Cade's mountain, and he had been a dead-shot since he'd been ten years old. Speed with a handgun, too, had come very easily, partly because he had the unexcelled, perfect co-ordination of youth, partly because Old Cade had told him, often, that when a man needed a gun he seldom had time to go looking for it, or to go groping for it.

But shooting was now a pastime. He had the cache of money he and Old Cade had squirrelled away each spring when they rode down and sold their winter-catch of pelts to Mister Farraday; in the uplands there was no way to spend money. Over the years the cache had grown considerably. Old Cade used to shake his shaggy head and smile, over that pile of silver. He had never cottoned much to the idea of just up and paying silver for things; that required no shrewdness at all. Barter was the best way. He'd said it many times, and he'd taught young Weldon all the ins and outs of bartering.

He rode off the stageroad, a mile to the east of it. That was another thing a man learned as a boy at another man's knee. Sheep and cattle and deer and goats followed someone else's trail; a bear and a panther and a man made their own way.

He rode, seeing the first pale green showing underfoot, seeing the snow-crested mountains thrusting sharp and brilliant in the morning sunlight. By the sun he guessed it to be no more than nine o'clock, a good time of morning to start out even if a man had no real destination, and that was what rode his spirit on this day. He had been around North Fork ten days. Excepting that bad interlude in the Montana House, he was now ten days older and had absolutely nothing to show for it. He had money, that wasn't his problem. He had bought the correct kind of clothing, and he had talked to all kinds of people, but there was no niche in North Fork, no place for him to settle in. It was beginning to seem as though he did not belong there.

The question that needed answering was: Where must he go?

He passed across a low-lying hump of land a mile down from the nearest brakes, the nearest fissures and gullies and serrated places before the foothills began. Over that round swell he had a good view of the tree-edge up ahead where sunlight spilled only in direct lines to the carpet of needles. From there, he reached the first trees, and felt better at once. It was an unconscious thing, but a man raised in the highlands never really felt right out on the open, naked prairie.

He crossed a moist small meadow head down, eyes moving. But there was no elk or bear sign, only the marks of deer. On ahead lay the peaceful place beside a creek-pool where he had done his practising before. It was far enough so that no one would hear him, and that mattered because a man felt foolish throwing stones into the air and bursting them with bullets, or fast-drawing against a low-dangling pine cone.

He passed through light and shadow, not making a sound, letting the horse have its head. He could never be lost in this kind of country. The *mountains* might get lost, but *he* never would. There were things a man from this kind of country knew from reading nature. Creeks always flowed in one direction. Mountain-folds led to trails and passes. Edible animals went high in summer and came low in winter.

The horse knew where they were going. He had only been up this way one other time, but because he hadn't been made to veer off either to the right or the left, he knew.

When they reached the park something low and heavy and ominously stealthy moved behind a chokecherry thicket. The horse did not notice but his rider did. As he swung to earth young Weldon called out an insulting epithet in Sioux and told the beast to leave. It did. It would have left anyway. It showed a fat rear-end covered with rough, dull hair. Bears leaving hibernation were not just ravenous, they were also mean. But this was a sow, a young sow-bear at that, and she had no wish to be near the two-legged thing. She left on a downhill lope that was clumsy and bumbling, because her fore-paws toed-in and she couldn't run quite straight.

Douglas Cade Weldon laughed at her, but his horse watched with a quivering lip. Of all the things horses feared, and that included just about everything, even wind-whipped scraps of paper, cougars and bears ranked foremost. Even the scent was usually enough to spook a horse out of his mind.

The sow went blundering through underbrush down the slope and was lost within moments. The horse still kept an eye in that direction, after his rider had loosened the cincha and slipped the bridle and hobbled him, so he could graze. The scent lingered.

Previously, young Weldon had practised shooting with a little wind; the pine cones had been swaying, which made it more interesting. Today, there was not a breath of wind, so it was like shooting from a stand, where the game did not move.

He spent fifteen minutes drawing without firing. He disciplined himself to it, because otherwise it seemed foolish. The gun sprang upwards when he touched it. There was no drag and no delay. Except for the little slitted thong tie-down that fit over the thumb-dog of the hammer, holding the weapon snug, it could have slipped

out of the holster just from bouncing when the holster moved at a walking horse's gait. It was, in young Weldon's opinion, a poor excuse for a pistol holster, except that down where men prided themselves on gun-handiness, it gave an edge a man might need if his life was on the line.

Then he practised on the lower-down pine cones again, sometimes banging away from a crouch, some-times twisting left or right as he drew and fired. But not once did he raise the Colt more than four inches after he'd drawn it. He had been taught to aim above and shoot below, to make a mastery of that kind of co-ordi-nation—eye and hand, hand and eye.

He never missed up close, which was tiresome, so he moved back almost to the limit of the gun's range— which was not great at all, and that disgusted him—not because he occasionally missed, or near-missed, but because it seemed silly to so foreshorten a pistol's barrel that all the range was sacrificed. Old Cade's dragoon pistol had a barrel nearly as long as a man's forearm. It was accurate for a long distance, better than a quarter-mile in fact, but this forty-five lost so much velocity and elevation at less than a hundred yards the bullets were sometimes six inches too low.

Well; in places where men fought close up, like that night at Clancy's saloon, the forty-five was a good enough weapon. As Stuart Campbell had said, a six-inch barrel is a hell of a lot quicker at clearing the holster than a twelve-inch barrel, and at a range of no more than twenty feet it was as deadly as a cannon.

But he would never take the thing hunting.

From his edge of vision he caught the horse flinging up its head. He whirled, thinking bear. It was a girl in a smoke-tanned, fringed riding skirt and boots. She was staring.

He straightened up slowly and blushed to the hairline as he holstered the gun. She had black eyes and a full, red mouth. She looked tall but that was probably because she was lithe and erect as she looked across the clearing at him.

He tried a weak smile. 'Just practising with a new gun, is all.' And as though that required more explanation he said, 'It's not much of a one, barrel's too short.'

She looked beyond him, then over where his horse was standing, then back. 'Aren't you Mister Weldon?'

He didn't know her from Adam's off ox. 'Yes'm. Douglas Cade Weldon.' If she was from town, why then that was probably where she had seen him. He hadn't seen her; if he had he would have remembered. He hadn't been around a lot of women but he'd seen some. Since coming to North Fork he'd seen more of them, but this was different. This was the kind of woman that if a man only saw her once, only spoke to her, like now, briefly in a forest glade, forever after as long as he lived she would be a young memory, something a man could recall in his last years as vivid and as unchanged.

'I'm Angeline Farraday, Mister Weldon.'

He acknowledged that to himself: Of course, she had the same black eyes, the same, but finer-textured, light-golden skin.

'My father has mentioned you, Mister Weldon.'

He hooked both thumbs in the shellbelt and loosened where he stood. He smiled at her. 'I reckon,' he assented. 'And I can figure about *how* he mentioned me.'

She considered that a moment before speaking again. 'You can explain that, if you'd like, Mister Weldon.'

He strolled over closer. 'I didn't mean anything, ma'm. Except that the trouble in the saloon makes things all different.'

She kept studying him a while longer. When he was closer, she said, 'I didn't mean to interrupt your shooting practice.' She smiled, with relief. 'I just heard all that gunfire and thought maybe someone might be hurt, up here. I was out riding.' She pointed. 'My horse is down there in the trees.'

They stood awkwardly together with a painful silence settling. He groped his way out of that. 'Nice day for riding.' He nodded in the direction of the chokecherry thicket. 'There was a bear yonder when I rode in. Reckon they're out, by now.'

She cast a fast look towards the bushes. 'That's why I stay out of the mountains when I'm riding alone.'

His brows lifted. 'Bears? They won't hurt you. Not if you let them know in plenty of time you're coming.

Well; there's a time of year when even a buck deer'll choose you, if you hang around too much. Usually, a person's a lot safer in the mountains than down in a town.' He bit his tongue. 'Well; *some* towns, I reckon. Not *your* town.'

She laughed at him. 'I don't care, Mister Weldon. You can say whatever you like about North Fork. I like it; I grew up there. But I have no illusions about it being paradise.'

She talked easily, effortlessly, once the self-awareness left her. She had just the right words, every time. She was the most beautiful girl he had ever seen. He couldn't even imagine one being more beautiful.

He retreated to safe ground again. 'Your paw is a fine man, ma'm.' He remembered something that might amuse her, and smiled as he related it. 'When I was younger I used to come down maybe once, twice a year, and stand in the doorway of his store, and afterwards, when I was home again, I'd lie awake at night thinking that must be what heaven was like. All sorts of new things, shiny and valuable and—well—shelves like that.'

Maybe she didn't think it was amusing because she looked at him without laughing. 'Did you always live up there with that old trapper, Mister Weldon? Wasn't it terribly lonely?'

'Lonely?' He pitied her. 'I've never been as lonely in the mountains as I've been in North Fork, ma'm. No, I didn't always live up there. I don't recollect too much from a long time back; I fell out of a wagon, hit my head on some ice, and when I came round again, the wagon was gone. My folks had seven other younguns.' He pulled a bitter grin at her. 'One less mouth to feed. Anyway, I guess they never came back . . . I went off on a trail and got so cold I figured I'd die. Cade was running a lower-down trapline and found me.' He finished that, drew a breath and twisted to look back. 'You don't know the mountains, do you?' He faced her. 'What you said about being afraid of bears . . . Someday, maybe we could ride up in there. I can show you things.' He stopped, shocked at his own boldness. 'Well; maybe I'd better catch my horse and head back for town.'

He turned without another word, without even a nod, and went out where his horse had grazed, to catch it and slip loose the hobbles, then to bridle it and cinch-up. When he turned, she was gone.

He stood a long time holding the reins looking down where she had been. Along with the sense of futility, of not-belonging, he now had a sense of peculiar restlessness.

One thing about being in the mountains, a man's thoughts and feelings were the same from day to day. Down on the plainlands, a man's feelings were based on reactions to things he did not appear to have much control over. Like that girl suddenly appearing out of nowhere, her appearance reaching deep down to stir him in a restless way.

He mounted, gave the horse its head, and until they broke out of the forest and he saw her loping far ahead, it did not occur to him how nice it would have been to ride all the way back to town with her.

SIX

A BAD NIGHT

The weather broke, wind whistled off distant snowfields, clouds gathered, the sunlight turned obscure through a high veil, and after a little more than two weeks of the springtime preview, winter was back.

It was of course only temporary, this biting, bleak cold with its wintery shadings, but temporary or not it drove North Fork back into hibernation. Wood smoke rode the late-day with the smell of mid-winter and people no longer stood along the walkways gossiping, or stood basking in good warmth anywhere at all.

Alex Farraday fired up his two big cast-iron stoves, one at each end of the big store, and when men congregated at Clancy's Montana House, they no longer made a beeline for the bar, they tarried first over where Clancy's woodbox stood, filled to the brim, near the stove.

People grumbled, as they did every year when this

happened. One taste of springtime spoiled everyone; made them impatient for the easy times of year, spring and summer. Douglas Cade Weldon was amused at Stuart Campbell. The gunsmith had already scratched the earth out back of his building—he lived in the pair of rooms behind the shop—had stirred in some black compost brought up the alley at some strain in a wheelbarrow from Ullman's barnyard, and had set out his seeds for the summer garden patch.

Now old Campbell was as testy as a bear with a sore behind because the ground might freeze, and if that did not kill his plantings it surely would retard them.

What amused young Weldon was that, although Stuart Campbell had to be heading well into his seventies, and therefore should have known, had probably seen this same thing happen fifty or sixty times, he still rushed the season like some impatient youngster. Sometimes it seemed that no matter how old people got, they still thought in the terms of youthful error. Maybe that was a good thing; maybe, if people ever got so that they knew in advance that haste made waste, they would just sit down and wait.

Young Weldon divided his time those first couple of days of cold and raw weather between Campbell's shop and Clancy's saloon. He had a trait which he had not yet recognized in himself; instead of loafing at the blacksmith shop or at the pool hall where other men his age hung out, Douglas Weldon lingered where there were older, not younger, men. It was an unconscious thing. He had grown from a cub to a full-fledged man acquiring the taciturnity, the habit of deliberation, the hard-won wisdom of an older man. He was most at ease with other older men. It was as natural for him to sit for long, silent periods at the gunshop or at Mike's bar, as it had been for him to sit the same way on winter nights up on Cade's mountain. A man did not have to talk all the time to prove he had a tongue, any more than he had to work hard to make people laugh.

A boy raised by an old man learns self-containment very early. That does not qualify him, very often, for the company of young men because he develops a gravity young men rarely have. But to compensate, a man like Douglas Cade Weldon had the kind of quiet, inner assurance that made the seeking of company just for its own sake, unnecessary.

He had a nickel beer the third night of winter's return at Clancy's bar, aware of the crowd but detached from it. He liked company, but it was nothing he had to have, and he only liked it at certain times.

No one attempted to use him as a butt for rough humour. Mostly, men were friendly, but with respect. Mostly, too, they were baffled. At least the young ones were; young Weldon *was* different. Clancy summed it up for the rangeboss of a cow outfit south of town by saying, 'His kind, you don't bully and they don't bully you.'

Then came the bad night for Dick Ullman, and if it wasn't exactly as Gabe Longstreet had predicted—it wasn't hell-raising cowboys, it was plain out-and-out renegades—the results were similar. Three of them had come up the alley in the bitter wind riding head-hung horses; and while one kept watch out front, another kept watch out back, the third one threw down on Ullman and his night-hostler and helped themselves to three fresh horses.

It was done professionally. There was no shooting and no great commotion and even when they struck down the nighthawk because he made a foolish move, it was done without passion. One of them simply crumpled the old man with a pistol-barrel across the skull.

By the time Ullman reached Clancy's place the outlaws were gone. Northward, Ullman said, red-faced and profane in his agitation.

It was a bleak night; folks had been predicting all day that before morning it would be snowing again. Ordinarily, two dozen riders would have rushed forth to give chase. Tonight, three itinerant cowboys volunteered, but otherwise men shuffled their feet and lingered in the good warmth.

Young Weldon finished his beer during Ullman's furious recitation. Then he looked over where the three rangeriders were sitting, decided they would do and jerked his head at them. If those horsethieves had gone north it would be into the mountains. There were no three men living who could evade Douglas Cade Weldon up there.

Ullman turned to watch as the cowboys arose in silence to follow young Weldon out of the saloon. 'You going after them?' he asked.

Weldon nodded at the door. 'Shouldn't take too long if those aren't mountain-wise horses they stole.'

Ullman glared around. 'Just the four of you? How about you other fellers?'

A man who rode Longstreet's coaches as gun-guard said, 'I been out in that weather every day now, and as far as I'm concerned someone else can have it at night.'

Ullman was indignant. 'I never figured I'd see the day . . . Well, by gawd you boys wait until I get my horse.' He turned angrily, and young Weldon barred the door shaking his head.

'You stay here, Mister Ullman.'

Dick stopped still. 'What?'

'You stay. Look after your hostler. We won't need you.' Ullman was momentarily nonplussed. He stammered. 'They're my horses, damn it all. Five men are better than four. I'll get a horse and meet you here in five—'

Weldon said, 'You stay—or I stay.'

That made it personal. Before, it had seemed Weldon had been thinking that since Dick was the local bone-setter and whatnot, he shouldn't leave town. Ullman's streak of meanness surfaced.

'Then I'll go,' he snarled, 'and you can stay.'

One of the silent cowboys sighed and headed back across towards the bar. Ullman interpreted that badly. 'Hey; you ain't going with me?'

The cowboy turned. 'Not me, Mister Ullman. With Weldon, we'll be back come morning. You aren't no mountaineer.'

The other two cowboys nodded and young Weldon, trying to smooth it over, said, 'There are four of us to their three, we'd do better like that than if we went up there sounding like an army.'

Ullman sneered. 'Naw, that ain't it. You don't like me, do you?'

Weldon considered, then shook his head. 'I don't, for a fact.' He looked at the three cowboys. 'Let's ride.'

Ullman stood helplessly by and let the four men depart. Afterwards, with almost everyone in the saloon suddenly finding the nude lady in Clancy's backbar painting deserving of their full attention, Dick Ullman stamped up and banged on the bar. As Clancy reached for a bottle and shot-glass, Ullman made a loud effort to salvage his pride by saying, 'Someday that whipper-snapper's going to push me too far.'

No one said a word.

As soon as young Weldon and his companions were mounted, were heading into the northward teeth of the bitter cold, the wonderful warmth that had accumulated in their clothing at the saloon, vanished. There were some stars, where rents in the black ragged clouds existed, but if the moon was up there no one could see it.

It was useless to try and talk in the face of the wind. Young Weldon felt no need for conversation, and around him the three cowboys seemed to be obeying an instinct that prompted them to their duty, but they weren't very happy about this, and weren't going to discuss it.

There was one thing the cowboys knew: No one could read signs on a night like this one was. But there was something else they knew: Douglas Cade Weldon was what the oldtimers called—among other things—a white Indian. When he'd acted confident back at the saloon doorway, that was good enough.

Then there was one basic fact: Those horsethieves, or whatever they were—outlaws of some kind at any rate—were heading north. They had a fair start, and after leaving North Fork would ride hard until they felt safe enough to pick a slower gait, so, for a couple of hours anyway, all the pursuing riders had to do was head in the same direction.

Once they reached the mountains it would be up to Douglas Weldon. Day or night, he would know how to handle things.

For Douglas Weldon, the time spent riding towards the foothills supplied the time he needed to think. Assuming those strangers did not know the land ahead they would rely on the darkness and the bleakness to help them. But also, being rangemen, at least being men in a range country and probably men who had lived like rangemen, they would not go foolishly riding up into mountainous country with which they were not familiar, to get lost, or to wear down their horses. They would stay to the stageroad.

Also, come firstlight they would know they had pursuit to deal with if the men from North Fork stayed to the road, and they would set up a neat ambush.

Near the brakes one of the cowboys, a lean, thin-lipped man, rode in close and said, 'I'd hole up until dawn if I didn't know this country.'

Douglas Weldon did not think so. 'If you figured a posse of men who *did* know the country, was out searching?'

The cowboy said no more. They passed across the broken country and where the road began its long lift, the wind lessened but the cold increased. The cowboys fished out their gloves and pulled down their hats. One of them swore with feeling, and also with chattering teeth.

Douglas Weldon gauged the distances; by now those outlaws would be conserving horse strength. By now too, they should be satisfied that even if pursuit were on its way, they were a satisfactory distance ahead of it. A walking horse carried a man a lot farther, in actual miles, than a running horse. If the outlaws had tapered off back at the base of the mountains, and if Weldon and his companions had been no more than perhaps two miles behind the horsethieves when they had left the saloon, then it was very probable that up ahead no more than another two miles, three at the most, the renegades were plodding along tucked up from the cold.

Weldon turned off the roadway and rode between two sentinel pines. Behind him, the cowboys did not even hesitate.

There was an ancient trail up through here. It was, in fact, a very good trail; once, this pathway had been the main route of that redskin highroad leading down to the prairie, and down across the exact spot where North Fork now stood. Douglas Weldon knew every yard of this trail. His destination was up under an immense black-rock bluff where the pass narrowed and the stageroad slipped through a cleft.

Up until now he had pushed the animals very little, but a half mile along, where the trail crossed a plateau, he loped without haste, and kept his horse at it for a full mile before hauling back down to a fast walk again.

Three times he did this, each time where the going was not steep, or at least not very steep. The cowboys came in his wake like three shadows, still not saying much although up in here there was no wind at all.

The moon broke through, unexpectedly, near the top-out, permitting an eerie moonscape of peaks and black pockets to show amid the bristle-topped pines and firs. Douglas Weldon twisted to look back, and grinned. The cowboys grinned back.

The last time they loped, the trail was swinging back towards the black-rock cleft. By Douglas Cade Weldon's most hopeful, but not *too* hopeful, estimate, he and his companions had to be at least a mile and a half ahead of the outlaws—providing those fugitives had not pushed their mounts dangerously hard, and had already crossed through.

But even if this had happened, it could only delay the return to town another few hours; men riding tired horses might hold a big lead for a while, but they could not do it forever. One way or another, the outlaws were living with a limited freedom.

SEVEN

CAPTURE AND RETURN

They did not come.

Weldon hunkered in the watery light and used a stick to make a tracing in the dirt. Below, a mile or perhaps a little less, was a turn-out, a place where freighters and stage-drivers could leave the road and rest their animals. Down there was a hollow-log water trough fed from a seepage spring. If the outlaws had decided to stop, that was Weldon's guess about where they might do it.

One of the cowboys wrinkled his brow in doubt. 'Unless they already cut up through here, and while we're wasting time they're heading down the far side.'

Weldon left the others back with the horses in a fringe of second-growth pines and reconnoitred the roadway. He came back to report that the outlaws were still below, somewhere. No one questioned his ability to read sign in the near-dark. These riders had been returning to the North Fork country for a number of years to hire out during the riding season. Since their most recent return they had heard all the news. They knew a lot about Douglas Cade Weldon. He was the kind of a man they respected.

When the outlaws still did not come, it never occurred to Weldon's companions to doubt that Weldon had missed the sign, down in the roadway, but one of them said, 'Just suppose them fellers *aren't* new to this country; they could have branched off on a trail like we done. Maybe over to the east.'

Weldon looked across the narrowing, low canyon, and looked back. 'If they did, they're still going to have to come back to the road. Those black-rock cliffs stretch for miles and this here is the only pass.'

The lank, turkey-necked man who had candidly said, back at the saloon, he would not ride with Dick Ullman, squatted and drew his coat close and, looking like a big stork in a Stetson, composed himself. The younger cowboys took their cue from this.

But it was a long wait, and that troubled everyone, including Douglas Weldon. It seemed incredible that

those fleeing outlaws would actually waste all this time. 'Rode down, I expect,' suggested the stork-like man. 'For all we know they done something a long way off and have been dodging posses for a week. Fresh horses aren't always a runnin' man's salvation.'

Weldon picked up the sharp but distant sound of steel over stone. On a bitterly cold night sound carried a long way. He did not comment, instead, he picked out the places and told the men to get down lower, closer to the road, and leave the horses up among the trees, but take Winchesters to the rock-jumbles above the road with them. The last cowboy to obey was the lanky one. He squinted hard over to the eastern slope, and shook his head. 'If they get into them damned rocks it'll take dynamite to smoke 'em out.' Then he turned and went down where his friends were spreading out, and grunted into place where the rocks felt like ice-blocks.

Douglas Weldon had already decided to stay a little higher. That way, if the outlaws tried to make a battle of it he would command both the road and the eastern slope. He would have a wider view.

But he did not expect a battle. Men had to be very desperate to try and draw against aimed guns they could not see.

The moon slid behind a waft of high vapour making this primeval upland world seem more ghostly, more other-worldly, than ever. Douglas Weldon looked, and felt like swearing. They were going to need the moonlight. Starshine alone would never be enough.

The vapour moved on, the moon soared again, and although it was only slightly more than half full, it was a lot better than no moon at all. In fact, from Douglas Weldon's high site, the view was excellent. He still did not make out the three-abreast horsemen until long after their sounds, their shod-horse noises and their hoarse voices, were clearly audible, but when they eventually came up out of the night heading into the narrow place ahead, he saw the grey horse first, then the two bay ones, settled the Winchester into a steady rest and waited.

The outlaws were buttoned into sheep-pelt coats and one even had a shawl round his head under his hat to keep his ears from being frost-nipped. Not a one of them had a carbine across his lap, but all three of them had their Winchester scabbards slung forward, butt-plates within inches of saddle-swells and handy to an unburdened fist.

That would not be good enough, though. Weldon remembered Stuart Campbell's emphasis on the length of barrel having everything to do with the speed of a draw. Carbine barrels were shorter than rifle barrels, but they were one hell of a lot longer than sixgun barrels.

Weldon ticked off the seconds, waited one additional moment until the outlaws on Ullman's animals were less than two hundred feet distant, downslope and almost parallel to him, then he called quietly.

'Stop where you are!'

They stopped; the horses, as astonished as the men, threw up their hands, but in a flash of movement the farthest man, perhaps gambling that there were no guns on the east slope, left his horse in a flinging leap—and two carbines slapped the night from lower down and the man, twisting in a run, went down with both arms outflung.

It was over in five seconds. The other two outlaws held both hands shoulder-high, the rein-hand and the carbine-hand. From closer to the road the turkey-necked cowboy drawled out for the outlaws to sit perfectly still. Then he unwound from hiding and walked ahead, carbine cocked and held one-handed, to disarm the prisoners.

Douglas Weldon eased down his firing-pin and moved into plain sight on his way down to the roadway. The other cowboys came out of concealment too. Their captives watched all this, then one turned and gazed downward where the third member of their crew was lumpy and still, on the frozen hardpan.

Weldon went over and, using the toe of his boot, eased that man over on to his back. He was dead. One of his friends said, 'Done for?' in a perfectly calm voice, and Weldon nodded. Then he picked up the corpse and slung it across leather. Without looking up he went to work using a lariat to lash the body fast. Turkey-neck went after the horses, and until he returned no one said anything. Then, however, the outlaw with the shawl around his head settled both hands atop the saddlehorn in an attitude of total defeat, studied the four men from North Fork, cleared his throat then spoke, 'How in hell did you boys get up ahead of us?'

Turkey-neck answered coldly. 'We flew. Open them coats and let's see if you got any hide-out weapons.'

This search netted one derringer, which was unloaded. Otherwise the outlaws had no other weapons. The cowboy from North Fork who had said the least all the way up from town, asked where the prisoners were from, and he got an answer he did not like.

'From the moon. What's the difference, you got us didn't you?'

The cowboy strolled over and reached with a thick arm to yank the flippant outlaw half out of the saddle. 'There are lots of trees in these hills, mister. You got any idea how folks use trees when they catch horsethieves?'

The outlaw grabbed for leather to keep his saddle, and his companion said, 'We're from Yellowstone. And before that, Cheyenne.'

'What you wanted for?' asked the cowboy, releasing his grip and stepping away so he could look up at the farthest outlaw.

'Who said we are wanted?'

The cowboy started around for that man. 'You're a pair of smart bastards, ain't you?'

The outlaw who had spoken, spoke swiftly to forestall the angry man moving in on him. 'All right. All right. We—got into a little ruckus and a couple of boys got hurt.'

Douglas Weldon got astride his horse. He waited for his companions to take their cue from this, then he motioned for the outlaws to turn, to head on back down towards the low country.

For the first time one of the outlaws began to doubt the legality of this capture. He narrowed his eyes at Weldon. 'You the law?'

Turkey-neck smiled. 'None of us are the law. But that ain't going to make one bit of difference, is it? Move out, herd the horse along with the dead feller on it. And shut up!'

There might have been an argument if Weldon or one of the others had been the town marshal, but these out-laws were knowledgeable rangemen: Provoking anger about now, especially with that quiet rider, the one who had evidenced a willingness to haul someone out of the saddle, looking flintily over, the prisoners obeyed Turkey-Neck to the letter. Neither said a word. The idea was simply that the law would not—at least it was not supposed to—countenance a lynching, but cattlemen were not always that predictable.

By the time they got down to the foothills again, and out where the wind still gusted, the outlaws seemed per-fectly willing to take their chances in a justice court in North Fork.

It was late, and it was cold, five or ten degrees colder

than it had been earlier, when Weldon and the others had ridden up into the canyon. It was past midnight by an hour or two.

Weldon rode hunched, as did the others. One passenger was not affected by the cold. He rocked along, head down on one side, feet down on the other side. When they were within sight of town, which showed only a few lights here and there, a cowboy leaned beside Douglas Weldon and said, 'What you reckon the chances are for a reward?'

It was a fair question; the cowboys had only recently arrived in the north country and had not as yet been hired on. Ordinarily, along about this time of year even the most frugal cowboy alive had been living on brush-rabbit stew and creek water for a month at the least.

Weldon had not thought about a reward. He had been riding along wishing that one damned fool hadn't tried to make a run for it. This would be the second time he'd got involved in trouble around North Fork, and a man had been killed. He was not too sure folks wouldn't think he'd shot that horsethief, even though he hadn't. It was pretty easy, evidently, to get a killer's reputation.

'I have no idea at all,' he said, about the reward. 'I wish that dead one hadn't tried to make a break for it.'

The cowboy looked at young Weldon. Then he straightened in the saddle and did not say another word. That look had reflected surprise; probably, after what the cowboy had heard about Douglas Weldon's double shootout in the saloon, he had expected the man at his side to be perfectly reconciled.

That was something worth reflecting about. If this man whom Douglas Weldon did not know, and who had not been in town at the time of the double killing, had been told the story of that battle in such a way that made Douglas Cade Weldon look like a professional gunhandler, then the person who had told him the story had undoubtedly believed Weldon *was* a willing gunfighter. If one person believed that, then it was reasonable to assume there were others who also did. So—even without returning from the pursuit with a dead man—folks were already making that judgment.

What would they be saying about Douglas Weldon tomorrow?

He was troubled more than depressed. The idea that had come to him before, that morning he'd ridden up to the poolside meadow to practise with the forty-five, came back. Maybe the best course for him, now, was to roll his blankets and go elsewhere.

In a new place he could put to use what he had learned in North Fork. In a new place he wouldn't even ride in carrying a gun.

'Someone's kept the light burning at the saloon,' one of the half-frozen cowboys said, pointing with a gloved hand. 'Bless his little old heart.'

Turkey-Neck and the others swung to the side as they entered town, called casually to Douglas Weldon they would save part of the bottle for him, and went directly to the Montana House's tie-rack.

Weldon herded the outlaws to the jailhouse, marched them inside, locked them all into the same cell without more than a nod at Johnathon Barlow, who had been awakened by the noise, and returned to the outer office where he dropped the key atop the old desk, then started for the door.

He had done everything he'd have done if he'd accepted that temporary marshal's job from the Town Council—and he would not get a dime for it, which did not bother him. What *did* come to mind though, was the fact that if he'd accepted the job as temporary town marshal what he had done tonight would have looked different, would have looked entirely justifiable.

EIGHT

THE DEAD MAN'S RETURN

By morning there was six inches of snow on the flat, and about a foot in the mountains. It would not stay; one day of sunshine and it would disappear, but when Douglas Weldon went out to have breakfast the world was white and clean, with no tracks.

A grey, low sky lingered though, so perhaps more snow would come. But it was warmer and the wind had departed, which was a blessing. Snow and cold were one thing, that frigid wind was another thing.

Gabe Longstreet was at the jailhouse when Douglas Weldon got down there to talk to Marshal Barlow. Under Barlow's supervision Longstreet, who was no stranger to letter-writing and log-entries, was taking care of the less strenuous but much more complicated business of legal paperwork. He and Barlow had found one of the outlaws on a wanted flyer out of Colorado. The dead one. There was a five hundred dollar reward. For the other two men there did not appear to be a legal demand, but all that meant was that Marshal Barlow's stack of wanted flyers was probably incomplete.

The prisoners sulked. When Weldon entered, they watched him with the malevolent hatred of a pair of crouching cougars. He ignored them.

Dick Ullman had claimed his horses the night before. He had also visited Johnathon Barlow earlier this morning. He had been impressed with Weldon's efficiency, and he had been glad to get his animals back, but he had told Barlow about the incident in the saloon, and now Barlow told Douglas Weldon that sometimes it was better in most ways to put up with little inconveniences than it was to make them grow out of proportion to their importance.

'If you'd taken him along, he'd have done as well as any of those rangeriders you took. If you're going to be around North Fork, you'll have to learn to live with Dick.'

Douglas did not make an issue of this. As far as he was concerned the fact that he had refused to ride with Ullman was a thing of the past. He did not even mention the one part of Barlow's talk that was pertinent to him, the part about being in North Fork. Whatever a man decided on something like that, he decided by himself.

Marshal Barlow seemed to be improving. He had lost a lot of blood and his wound, having been a ragged one, would require a lot of healing, a lot of time. Around town there were still people who said he would not make it, but the ones who visited him every day or two, could see definite improvement. He did not tire so readily, nor drowse off in that weak lethargy that had been indicative of his condition the first week or two, and his appetite was improving. He still could not sit up, and as Gabe Longstreet told Stuart Campbell and Douglas Weldon, in the gun shop, he was still a very long way from standing or walking, but if there was no set-back, Johnathon Barlow ought to be able to get back to work, perhaps, before the end of summer.

The reason Gabe was there, at old Campbell's gun shop, was because North Fork was still without a peace officer, and more than ever people had things to say about this, after Ullman's hold-up, and after his night-hostler had died from the blow on the head one of those horse stealing outlaws had given him.

Gabe—and Ullman too, now—wanted Douglas Weldon to re-consider. Old Campbell listened, kept working at his bench, and smiled a little, but took no part in the talk.

Weldon would not have taken any part in it either, if there had been a way not to, but he was not rude by nature so he stood and politely listened to all Longstreet's pleas, and shook his head.

'You can find other men,' he said. Then he showed how his thoughts had been running lately by saying, 'I may not be here much longer anyway.'

Longstreet turned to old Campbell for support, but all he got there was an enigmatic little smile, and silence.

But after Longstreet left the shop Stuart Campbell said, 'You got some idea it isn't right for a man to make his calling other people's troubles. Well; I can see that. But to a feller who growed up on the mountain with only one other person around, things are a heap simpler than they are down here.'

Douglas smiled. 'That's a fact.'

Campbell went on speaking. 'When a man's pretty much alone, he's only got to look after himself. But when folks all gang together like sheep, in a town, why then they got to have rules, otherwise a man wouldn't das't step outside at night or someone'd shoot him for his hat, maybe, or his boots. So—you got to have laws—and you got to have men who'll enforce 'em. That's about the size of it, Douglas. You can't be among folks and still figure everything's the same as it was up there in the mountains.'

Later, that same evening, with an early dusk coming, as though it were still mid-winter, when Douglas Weldon went down to Ullman's to see about stabling his horse there, because the public corral north of town had no shelter, he did have quite the same argument put to him, but Dick Ullman did make one valid point. He said, 'Folks help you, if you're sick, or badgered by outlaws like I was, and if them things happen to *them,* why it's a man's duty to do the same . . . Sure, you can bring the horse down. I got an extra stall and some empty corrals.'

The best of all these talks, though, came unexpectedly, when Douglas Weldon appeared before closing time at the *Emporium.* After he had bought some woollen socks and a blue bandana neckerchief, Alexander Farraday, who acted subtly different towards him, for some reason Weldon could not guess, said, 'Gabe Longstreet told me you turned him down again on the marshal's job. Every man has his reasons, of course, and I reckon every other man ought to respect them. But I've been thinking, this afternoon. Suppose we formed a vigilance committee here in town, to sort of keep the lid on until Johnathon's back on his feet—would you ride with it? What I've got in mind is that there's no one around who knows the mountains like you. Whenever North Fork has been hit by outlaws or law-breakers in the past, they never headed out across the prairie, they headed into the uplands. I can tell you damned few have ever been brought back once they got up in there. Would you do that, ride with the vigilance committee?'

Douglas said he would think about it, and left. On the way to the hotel in the gathering gloom, he met Angeline on her way past to the store. She smiled quickly and easily, as though they were old friends, and complimented him on bringing back Ullman's horses and the men who had stolen them.

He reacted to her presence as he had that other time, with a feeling of pleasurable discomfort. 'They just didn't know the country,' he responded, then shunted that topic out of the way. 'Just talked to your father, at the store.'

She put her head slightly to one side and gazed at him. 'I can guess what about. He and the others want you to help out until Mister Barlow is well. But you won't do it.'

He smiled. 'Word gets around.'

'North Fork is a small town, Mister Weldon. There really isn't much news, ever, so people have to talk about other people.' Her black eyes twinkled. 'If it's harmful, it's called gossip, otherwise it's called a discussion.'

He knew little about that fine distinction, and he cared even less. When she smiled her eyes brightened in a way that sang across to him. While he admired her he said, 'You maybe figure I'd ought to take the job.'

'No,' she replied slowly, picking the words. 'No; but probably for different reasons than some people. I just don't want to see you end up walking the roadway with a tied-down gun looking for trouble even if you have to manufacture it.'

'Gunfighter? Barlow didn't turn into one.'

'Marshal Barlow is an older man, Mister Weldon. He has lived differently than you have.'

That didn't make much sense to Weldon. 'Whether folks live different or not, ma'm, they know right from wrong. A man can carry a gun—most men do—but that doesn't mean he's got to go round proving he's good with it.'

She kept looking at him. When he finished she said, 'Do you like to ride in the cold? I do. I'm going riding tomorrow up towards the foothills. I'd like it if you'd come along, Mister Weldon.'

This was something he never would have had the boldness to suggest, but that did not impede his willingness to accept when *she* suggested it. 'Be right proud to. When?'

She hung fire a second, then said, 'Ten o'clock in front of the public corral at the upper end of town?'

He would be there, he told her. When they parted and he trudged away he thought that he would be there if he had to crawl up the centre of the roadway down on all fours.

Later, after supper, when he went down to the Montana House, Mike Clancy nodded a grinning greeting and swept both hands under the bar to draw off a nickel beer. Douglas was cultivating a taste for beer. It was not only less cutting to drink, it did not produce the same effect if a man kept drinking it. It was also five cents a big glassful as opposed to Clancy's hard liquor, which was ten cents a tiny shot-glass full.

Old Campbell ambled in, which surprised even Clancy. In the years since Clancy had operated his saloon, the gunsmith had been inside for a drink no more than a dozen times. Later, as the customers began drifting in from the night, Gabe Longstreet also appeared, then Alex Farraday, and still later, when the place was humming and alive with the activity of rangeriders, too, Dick Ullman arrived. All of these men, with the exception of Stuart Campbell, were steady patrons.

All old Campbell said by way of explanation when he settled against the bar at Weldon's side, was: 'Damned sight warmer here then down at my diggings.' Clancy set him up a bottle and a glass, and the gunsmith made a ceremony out of pouring, sampling, then drinking, his sour mash whiskey. He never jumped right into a conversation. Like Old Cade had done, Campbell made a kind of prolonged ritual of anything serious he had to say.

Douglas waited. He understood the exact protocol of all this, even though he did not know—and never was really very curious about why—old men did this, but he knew precisely what his role was, and leaned, drank his beer, gazed at the sparkling array of Clancy's bottled inventory on the backbar shelves, and waited.

Eventually old Campbell said, 'You pondered much on Alex Farraday's scheme of organizing a citizen's vigilance committee, Douglas?'

Weldon waited a dignified moment before answering; 'Nope.' The truth was, since meeting Angeline Farraday he hadn't once recollected that earlier conversation with her father. Nor much of anything else, either, for that matter. 'Some reason why I should have, Mister Campbell?'

'Yes.'

Weldon looked around and down. Campbell was meticulously refilling his shot-glass with a hand as steady as stone. He knew he was being looked at but until he had put the bottle aside, had snugged the glass closer in a claw-like scarred, wrinkled hand, he held his silence.

'That outlaw that got himself killed up in the pass, Douglas, the night you and them cowboys run down the horsethieves . . .' Old Campbell hoisted the shot-glass and dropped its contents straight down. He clenched his fist round the glass, batted his eyes, then blew out a shaky breath. 'That gawddamned likker was just made yesterday,' he gasped. 'Clancy is a miscreant for peddlin' this poison.'

'What about that outlaw. Mister Campbell?'

'His name wasn't Anderson, like it said on the reward

poster, Douglas, and he wasn't just wanted in Colorado for robbing coaches and banks. His name was Charley Benton and he was one of the Benton brothers who've been notorious throughout the southwest for ten years. He was the youngest, the baby of the litter.' Campbell pushed both bottle and shot-glass away, twisted and looked up as he talked on. 'When the request for the reward went through, folks down south was pleased that, finally now, one of the Bentons ain't going to kill and rob no more. But his brothers are on their way.'

Douglas returned old Campbell's steady look. 'To North Fork?'

'Yup, to North Fork. Now then, son, that talk you made about maybe riding on—you really mean to do it? Because if you do, why then I'd advise you to saddle up this very night. Don't put it off until daylight, for then you'd have to see the looks on folks' faces. No one would think too much of a feller gettin' their town into this kind of a fix, then riding on. You understand?'

Douglas scowled. 'Hell; *I* didn't kill that outlaw.'

The gunsmith nodded gravely. ' 'Course you didn't, son. You know that and I know it, and most folks around town know it too. But have you seen them rangeriders who went up the pass with you that night, the last day or two?'

Douglas hadn't.

'They're gone, boy. They pulled stakes last night when the word first come that the outlaw they killed was one of the Bentons. Now then—who does that leave? You.'

NINE

RETURN OF THE SUNSHINE

I t did not all fall into place until he and Angeline Farraday were riding up through a sparklingly golden, but cold, morning, the next day, and when he rode along at her side lost in solemn thought without speaking for almost an hour, or until they reached the foothills with the snow magically disappearing behind them, back in the direction of town, she finally asked him his thoughts, and he said, 'I'm having trouble figuring people out. Last night Stuart Campbell told me that dead horsethief was a wanted man with a couple of brothers who are on their way to North Fork.'

'Why should that be so difficult to understand?' asked Angeline. 'The brothers want to—'

'That's not what I don't understand,' said Douglas. 'Yesterday your father and Mister Longstreet asked again if I'd take Mister Barlow's place until he could be up and around again. I told them I wouldn't. Last night Mister Campbell told me of the coming of the Benton brothers, and said if I was going to ride on, I should do it now, before the Bentons got here . . . Well; don't you see? They knew the Bentons were coming night *before* last, and yet they didn't say it right out to me, until *last night.*'

Angeline turned out to know more than she had indicated, thus far. 'They did not want to force you; did not want to make it look as though you *had* to take the marshal's job. I heard my father and Mister Longstreet talking in our kitchen after supper last night. They had been to see Stuart Campbell. They, and Mister Ullman, and some of the other men around town. They didn't want someone you hardly knew, or maybe someone you didn't care much for like Mister Ullman, to explain things to you. At first, Mister Campbell refused. Later, he agreed. So, they were at the saloon last night when he told you.'

Douglas looked at Angeline as she told him all this. He kept looking at her afterwards, too. 'Did *you* know, when we met down near the store yesterday?'

'No. Not then. But about an hour later I knew.' She faced forward in the saddle as they entered the lower-down fringe of forest. 'And it kept me from sleeping very well, too.' She reined in and out where the snow still lay, where morning warmth, increasing slowly out on the prairie, had melted all the snow by now, but where the warmth could not penetrate fully among the trees until late afternoon, and set their course for the little park up ahead that had the creek-fed pool of clear water. She did not say any more until, just before reaching her destination, she pressed with one palm on the cantle and twisted to look back.

'Mister Weldon—people aren't *supposed* to be any different singly, or whether they come in bunches, except that in bunches it's harder to understand them, sometimes.' She smiled at him, then faced ahead and rode on up to their little meadow, where sunlight had reached straight down to melt the snow.

He watched her, wondering how to make her stop calling him Mister Weldon. Maybe, if he set an example by calling her Angeline. But he winced at that, not because he wouldn't have liked to call her Angeline, but because, since arriving in North Fork, he had come up against something, subtle but solidly underlying most intercourse among the people in town, that Old Cade had neglected to instruct him about: Social etiquette.

The small meadow with its pond was the first really warm place they had encountered. Even out on the range, because it had been early in the new day, the heat had not been very noticeable. Still, it had been very pleasant to get out of bed at the hotel this morning to find sunshine outside instead of more bleak weather.

They let their horses wander and strolled to the side of the pool, which was really no more than that. It was about twenty feet across and perhaps fifteen feet long from where the snow-water creek tumbled down out of the forest into it, at the north end, and overflowed from it at the south end. He showed her how the pool had been made originally. Beavers had dammed it at the lower end. There was little left to show where the dam and the beaver nest had been, now, except for the mound of flotsam that had been washed down each spring to lodge against the original dam.

'Trapped out,' he explained, pointing to the dam where he read the sign. 'Maybe fifty years ago.'

She said that was sad. 'It's such a beautiful little meadow.'

He did not deny this, but he had grown up trapping, so his outlook was different. 'Men take what they have to, otherwise they don't have any way to get money.' He did not justify trapping except to explain it this way. Then he took her up the creek and showed her dew-claw marks where a large, heavy elk had passed through no more than an hour earlier. 'Buck,' he exclaimed. 'Big and old and tough as a boot.'

She looked from him to the faint mark in the moist earth. 'How do you know it was a buck?'

He blinked at her. 'Dew-claws. Cow elks don't have 'em.' He grinned indulgently. 'You've missed some educating. See where the marks turn almost together. He was old. Old elks are tough to chew. See how deep he sank? He was big and heavy.'

She looked, then she smiled. 'I can tell you something about it, too.'

'What?'

She laughed. 'He was thirsty. That's why he was here at the creek.'

He grinned. 'You'd make a good partner.'

She turned away, ran a slow glance elsewhere, then said, 'Are you really going to leave?'

He followed her over to a big, punky old deadfall-pine across the clearing at the edge of the forest. When she sat down he sat beside her looking up through the dark forest.

'Wouldn't be right, would it? Isn't that what those fellers were trying to get across to me last night?'

'What they were trying to get across to you last night, Mister Weldon, was that the decision is yours; but they wanted you to know how *they* felt, and what may happen if you stay.'

He tipped back his hat. 'The Bentons arriving?'

'Yes.'

He was not worried about that. 'Kind of like a marauding old boar-bear isn't it? There's not a lot a man can do to prevent them from entering his hunting territory. But once he gets there, why then the man does whatever he's got to do to protect his territory.'

She said, 'Mister Weldon—bears don't shoot back.'

He smiled and turned to face her. 'You figure I'd ought to ride on?'

She sat looking into his eyes and saying nothing. No woman ever liked the idea of someone facing death, perhaps being killed through violence. Then she dropped her eyes and moved slightly so that she could see where the horses had got to in their browsing. 'If you ride on

Mister Weldon, at least the Bentons won't kill you.'

'They shouldn't really want to, ma'm, since I'm not the man who killed their brother. But those cowboys left in a hurry, and that leaves me . . . and if I pull out too, that'll leave Marshal Barlow, weak as a kitten with a ruined left arm, and Stuart Campbell, who's too old for fighting any more, and the others—Clancy, Longstreet, your paw.' He watched a saucy chipmunk with a striped back hop on the far end of the deadfall and eye them. 'That'd be their vigilance committee, I reckon. The only one I'd guess could shoot straight is a seventy-year-old man. Seems likely to me, ma'm, that two real gun-fighters could chew up the lot of them without having to work at it very hard.' He smiled. 'Stuart Campbell says a man in a town's got a debt he owes everyone else. I'll stay.'

'You don't owe North Fork anything, Mister Weldon.'

'No, maybe not,' he drawled, then surprised her by saying. 'Tell me something I don't know who else to ask about: When a man talks to a woman and figures he knows her, can't he call her by her given name?'

She almost smiled at him. 'He can.'

'Well—can't *she* do that too, if she figures she knows a man?'

Angeline looked down at the grass in front of their log. '. . . Douglas?'

A big sassy bluejay came swooping, saw them and

85

dug at the air in a frantic effort to gain altitude. He also screamed his raucous warning, the way bluejays usually did when they found people where people by natural rights did not belong. The cry of alarm was to warn every other animal.

It was a pleasant relief for the man and woman on the log in the warm sunshine. He had no idea how Angeline was feeling, but Douglas Weldon knew for a fact he was beginning to feel uncomfortable and slightly troubled. It was easy, as long as they talked about that old elk who had recently passed through, or even the Benton brothers, for him to be with her. But the moment they talked about each other, things changed.

The chipmunk fled like a wind-blown leaf, after the bluejay's cry. Even their horses looked up and around. Weldon watched the bird's flight up into the forest where its outcries grew fainter, and said, 'Pesky things. I've had 'em runoff game right under my nose.'

Angeline seemed relieved to have this neutral ground for their conversation, too. 'But he's very colourful. And he's only trying to protect the other animals.'

There was no denying either of these statements, but not every hunter who had been frustrated by the sharp eyes and the interfering tactics of bluejays could suddenly, on the spur of the moment, forgive all those exasperating transgressions. Douglas Weldon listened until the bird was long gone, did not argue against the 'jay, and did not agree either.

Angeline said, 'Do you know whose idea that was, about the vigilance committee?'

Weldon knew. 'Sure. Your father's.'

'Mine. I told him what I thought they should do, and it wasn't because I had heard you might leave North Fork, it was because I felt they had no right to ask any one man, no matter how good he might be with guns, to have to face down professional killers like the Bentons.'

He thought about that. If she had explained it differently, he would have been happier. But of course there was no reason for her to want to help him, any reason why she should have him in mind, at all, Bentons or no Bentons.

'Douglas?'

'Yes'm?'

'. . . Nothing.' She arose and brushed old bark off, then walked out where the heat was making their horses drowse all loose-legged and head-hung.

He watched her. Old Cade had once said, of the relationship between men and women, that it wasn't the same with people as it was with animals, and that it made no difference whether the man was a cabin-dweller and the woman a tipi-dweller; what mattered most of all was that, even in their silences, they shared the same needs and the same thoughts. *That,* he had told young Weldon, was what made something good out of something that more often than not, did not survive one long winter.

She turned, leaned across her horse's back and smiled. He was still sitting on the old log. He was gazing out there with a very grave expression. She called to him. 'We'd better start back . . . Douglas? Will you do something for me?'

He stood up and went slowly forward. 'I reckon. Leave North Fork?'

'No. Come to dinner tomorrow night.'

He gave no answer until he was out there with her, with the horses. 'Well; maybe I shouldn't.'

She was interested at once. 'Why not?'

'Well; your paw . . .'

'What about him?'

'Well. I don't reckon he'd like it, that's why.'

She said, 'My father likes you, Douglas. He—I don't think he nor any of the others can understand you, but they like you.'

Weldon thought of Dick Ullman, but he did not mention him. He helped her get the horses ready, and as he watched her step lightly up to the saddle, he agreed to come to dinner, but the moment he had accepted he began to feel wretchedly unsure.

She probably sensed this because as they rode down from the little pleasant meadow she talked of things that should have made him feel more confidence in himself, mentioned things she was sure would make him smile.

But they didn't. All the way back to town he regretted that she had asked him to dinner, and he regretted even more that he had accepted. The last thing he thought, just before they entered town by the north stageroad, was the same thing he had thought before: It sure was a lot different, a lot harder, living down here in North Fork, than it had ever been in the mountains. Down here, things happened to a man he did not really have a defence against.

Love was one of them.

TEN

A DIFFERENT ANGELINE

Old Campbell said, 'Folks got ways of knowing, that's about all I can tell you, son. Maybe, when they heard their brother got killed up here, maybe they went up and told some lawman they were going to ride north and settle up for that. Go ask Johnathon Barlow. If it come from anywhere, it must have been there.'

Campbell was right. Johnathon was drinking beef broth one of the ladies had brought in. It was salty and it was hot, but there was nothing as good to make blood as beef broth, everyone knew that, so Marshal Barlow sat propped up and drank it while he listened to Douglas Weldon. Then he said, 'It was bound to come out anyway, because an application for the reward would make it general knowledge down south. After that, you can bet the Bentons sounded off in a card game, maybe, or at a bar. After that, well, it would get back to some peace officer. Anyway, it was in the letter that come back from Cheyenne that they were coming.' Barlow finished the broth; it had to be drunk hot because otherwise, if it cooled, all the grease rose to the top and formed a slippery film. He put the big cup aside and made a face. 'You know something Mister Weldon? It come to me a few days ago that if a sick man recovers, he damned well might do it in *spite* of his well-wishers, not *because* of them.'

Douglas smiled. 'You're looking better.'

'Feeling better too,' agreed Barlow, and eased back to put a sombre look on his visitor. 'You could still ride out, you know.'

Weldon looked into the adjoining cell, which was empty. Gabe Longstreet had sent the surviving pair of outlaws in chains and under armed guard, down to Cheyenne where they were wanted for bank robbery and murder. 'No I can't, Marshal. Well, maybe if all that was involved was saddling and bridling a horse, I could do it. But that's not what's involved, is it?'

'Don't risk getting killed for a town that owes you nothing, Douglas. Let me tell you something: Maybe you're faster with a gun than either of the Bentons—but there are two of them. And that's not all. From what I've read-up on the Bentons, they are smart and damned well experienced. It'll be altogether different than it was at

Clancy's bar that night, with the orry-eyed cowboys. And there's even more: I know about this vigilance committee. I've been through that other times, in other places. Ain't a merchant living that's worth a damn as an ally in a gunfight. Not a solitary one. You're going to have to face those two gunmen alone. All right; the vigilance committee will be there, in the hotel windows and maybe in the doorways of their stores—but they aren't going to be in the roadway with you, and that's where it's all going to come un-strung.'

'You want me to slope, Marshal?' Weldon asked quietly.

Barlow was honest in his answer. 'I wish to hell I knew *what* I wanted. I sure don't want to be responsible for getting you killed. And I don't want the town burned or shot up, or maybe have some of the folks shot down in broad daylight by some ambushing outlaws sneaking into town by a back alley.' Barlow looked at his weak and injured body. 'I wish to hell I could stand up, just for a half-hour, when they get here.'

Weldon stood up. 'You're that sure they are coming?'

Barlow nodded and did not speak. He just nodded his head, but the look on his face gave all the support that head-nod needed. Barlow believed without a single shred of a doubt, that the Bentons were coming.

Weldon went to the hotel to clean up before going down Elm Street—which had five cottonwoods the length of it, and nary a single elm tree—to the Farraday residence. He killed all the time he dared, then he set out for the supper engagement clean and shiny, and miserable with self-consciousness and dread for fear he would do, or say, something wrong.

Angeline met him at the front door. Her father was being detained at the store, she told him, but he wouldn't be long. She was wearing a white dress that fit snugly across the chest and down at the waist, then flared a little and fell gracefully to within inches of the floor. She had her very dark hair caught close in back and tied with a little yellow ribbon. She was the prettiest thing he had ever seen; pretty, in fact, as a dainty little yearling doe.

He let her take his hat. Here, in these surroundings, she had him at more of a disadvantage than ever. Also, she was more natural, here, than she'd been when they'd ridden to the meadow. She settled him in a deep leather chair, then she left and very shortly returned with a thick glass of beer.

'It's terrible,' she said, making him look at the beer, thinking she meant the *beer* was terrible. 'My mother never allowed spirits in the house, and I ought to be ashamed, fetching you a glass like this. The women around town, if they could see this . . . Well . . .'

He understood. Although he had matured not thinking any evil at all was in strong drink, by now he had learned, around North Fork, that most folks felt otherwise. At least *womenfolk* thought so, and some of the men *said* they thought so, but he'd also seen them bellying up to Clancy's bar. He knew what a hypocrite was, but that is not what those men were. All the time they were denouncing the Demon Rum, rolling up their eyes and looking sanctimonious enough for butter to melt in their mouths, there was a sly little discernible twinkle in their eyes.

He tasted the beer to be certain his first notion hadn't been right. It hadn't, the beer was good. He raised his eyes, saw her slight blush, and leaned to put the glass on a little marble-topped table near at hand.

'Angeline? If a man was to settle here. I mean, after the Bentons come and go. If a man was to settle here, and get some kind of work . . .'

'Yes, Douglas?'

He never finished. He picked up the glass and drank deeply, astounded at his boldness. So astounded, in fact, that when he rolled his eyes around at her over the top of the glass, whatever else he had meant to say, blanked out in his head and he could not, for hell or high-water, remember a word of it.

Her father arrived. Douglas was on his feet in an instant, hand extended. Alex Farraday grasped the hand, a blank look passing over his features just ahead of a smile. He had been greeted as though young Weldon had been counting the moments before Farraday arrived.

Angeline vanished to the back of the house. Her father dropped into a chair, propped his feet on a little stool, and in a way that seemed very different from his manner at the *Emporium,* said, 'There are times when I wish to hell I'd gone into almost any other business.' Then, when Angeline returned bearing a second thick glass mug of beer, Farraday looked up with his black gaze soft, and took the glass. 'Thank you, angel,' he said, his gaze lingering in fondness. 'What did you learn at the Ladies' Altar Society today?'

Angeline laughed. 'That no one knows how to crochet except Belinda Longstreet. Everyone else does it wrong, even Mrs. Leatherman who has been doing it for fifty years. Have your beer, then go wash. Supper is almost ready.' As she turned to sweep out of the room, Angeline's dark eyes caught Douglas Weldon's gaze, and held it, then she left.

Alex Farraday's interest in Douglas Weldon was different in his home than it was at the store. It had to be of course; Douglas was not here at *his* invitation, nor to see *him.* A man with only one child, a daughter, mandatorily viewed young men in his house as something more than casual passers-by.

Douglas, without having been through this before, could understand it, had, in fact, thought it would be about like this when Angeline had extended the invitation, and now, even though her father acted perfectly natural and was affable, for Douglas it was an awkward time.

Later, when they went out to the dining-room, he was alert to Alex Farraday's deportment and manners,

copying nearly everything, and afterwards all he remembered of the meal was that Angeline was a good cook, it had all been filling and tasteful, but just exactly what he had eaten he could not remember, not right then at any rate.

They talked at the table. The Bentons were not mentioned. Nor was the fight at Clancy's saloon. Nor was the pursuit of those outlaws who had stolen Ullman's horses. They discussed North Fork as a community, and a dozen other easy topics. Alex Farraday remembered Old Cade and related anecdotes about Cade's visits to town. Douglas, who was the real authority on this topic, smiled and listened to what Farraday recalled, and drank coffee without saying very much about Old Cade.

Angeline knew how to keep a conversation from dying, which was fortunate because, actually, Douglas did not have much small-talk. Unless of course someone chose to bring up trapping or hunting or exploring mountains, and down around North Fork those were not common subjects, except in the fall of each year when everyone who was able, took a rifle and went hunting in the hills.

Angeline, Douglas noticed, seemed to know when one topic was wearing thin; she would have another one to strengthen the conversation with. By the end of their supper he was a little awed by her poise and talents. Afterwards, when he and her father went back to the parlour and Alex Farraday lit a fragrant cigar, it did not seem that Angeline was out back more than fifteen minutes, then she appeared looking as fresh and beautiful as though she had not been working like a slave all afternoon and evening.

Alex Farraday had to examine some invoices he'd brought from the store tonight. He told Douglas that when a man owned his own business the main reward was that he got to sit up until midnight several nights a month keeping ledgers, and otherwise he got to do all the worrying. Farraday laughed and excused himself.

Angeline stood by the fireplace when Douglas told her the dinner had been one of the best he'd ever tasted.

She said, 'You didn't eat much.'

He thought he had, so her remark surprised him. 'Enough to founder a horse.' He arose and strolled over to also stand with his back to the fire. 'You look different tonight.'

She laughed. 'I'm not dressed for riding, is all.' She looked up into his face. 'You look different too, Douglas.' He did not think he could possibly look *very* different. But he said nothing and the silence threatened to settle between them. She had been forestalling this all evening. By now she could almost predict when he would go quiet.

'Have you ever been down the river in a canoe?' she asked. When he shook his head she said, 'I have one in the bushes down at the riverbank, and I was thinking about taking a joy-ride tomorrow. It would be more fun if you'd come along.'

He had been on a big body of water only once in his life. That had been when he and Cade had had to cross an icewater lake one time many years back when they'd had a trapline about fifteen miles deep through the mountains. Cade did not care for large bodies of water. Anyway, the trapping was better beside little creeks. Douglas knew how to swim, Cade had insisted that he learn that, but he had never gone out on the water for pleasure, and he knew nothing about paddling canoes.

She waited for him to speak and when he didn't she said, 'This time of year with the trees leafing out and the water the same colour as the sky, it's beautiful.'

He nodded about those things. Instantly she said, 'Wonderful; I'll meet you down at the riverbank about ten o'clock. Walk straight down from behind the Montana House. The canoe is in almost a direct line from there.'

He looked at her, turning slightly wary. Her dark eyes were quick and bright, which meant she was not at all slow-witted. But sometimes he got the impression she was just a trifle *too* quick-witted.

When it came time for him to leave she went out on to the veranda with him, and when they were standing close above the stairs and their hands touched, he closed his fingers round her hand without speaking. They stood like that for a long time, silent, acutely aware of one another, then he freed her and stepped down one step before turning back to tell her, again, what a wonderful supper it had been. She looked him in the eyes from the same level, her mouth soft and her eyes gentle.

'I'm glad you came, Douglas. I wanted you to, very much. Good night.'

He knew what he wanted to do. He even thought she wanted him to do it, too. The turmoil was terrible. He controlled his expression, said, 'Good night, Angeline,' and turned to step the rest of the way down the stairs and turn west, which was to his left, for the walk back to the centre of town where the hotel was.

ELEVEN

BLISS ON IMPULSE

Anyone with a sound sense of balance could manage in a canoe. The trick, Douglas discovered, was to get into one, and get out again, without capsizing the frail craft. He got in after watching how Angeline managed it, and later, he got out the same way, by watching where she put her feet, and placing his the same way.

Paddling was a little more difficult to master. After the sweep backwards, which propelled the canoe ahead, a paddler turned his paddle sideways, flat to the side of the canoe, and then pushed it away, or held it close, depending upon how the canoe was to be steered. Angeline was very experienced. She also surprised Douglas by having a powerful thrust. She was a lot stronger than he would have thought.

Current was a factor particularly at this time of year when springtime thaws in the back-country made all the little tributary creeks run fast and cold. Normally, it would have been impossible to paddle a canoe upriver, although it went downriver with ease. Angeline explained that if they remained close to the bank, in the quieter shallows, they would have no trouble returning upriver. Douglas hoped she was right, because within an hour they had scooted southward about five miles.

That far from town it was as though they were the only people on earth. Willows and cottonwoods hid the view of North Fork, and elsewhere there were cattle and a few deer, even a loping coyote or two, but no people. Not even any horsemen. The cow outfits would not really begin working their herds for another few weeks; not until the ground firmed up, the sunshine was to be relied upon, and the last danger of a freak storm was past.

Angeline showed Douglas a small brushy island, and on its south side a quiet pool filled with fish. But they had no poles and no lines or bait. She let the canoe get caught in the current and steered it masterfully to the far shore where a strip of white sand made a beach. Here, she took him ashore and showed him all that remained of an old adobe house.

As soon as she said it had been a fort, 'way back, he remembered Cade telling of a time he and three other Mountain Men had been driven into this mud building, which had been a trading post and cache for early-day trappers, by a whole tribe of irate Indians, bucks, squaws, and even pups, who had wanted the newcomers out of their hunting grounds.

He told her of that episode and she said she had heard the story before, from that old hostler the horsethieves had killed. He had been there too.

They walked out where new green was flourishing, where deep wallows made by bull buffaloes were still as fresh-looking, and as deep, as though they had been made only last month.

They watched a straggling little band of elk heading north to the uplands for the summer, and when a pair of flashy black and white magpies scolded from a safe distance, they talked back to them. And they laughed.

The sun was warm, the air was as clean as though it had just rained. There was a smell to springtime a person never found any other time of year. It was part perfume, part mould. It seemed to promise much more than Douglas could hope to understand, the same way clear stars did on cold nights.

They walked back hand-in-hand. She was less talkative than usual but when he looked, she met his gaze with a gentle sweetness, which was enough; there were times when words were inadequate; there were times when it was better to say nothing.

Big trout rolled along the surface of the river, and although it was past feeding time, they still jumped after winged insects now and then.

The creek-willows that grew upon both banks were already noisy amid their topmost branches where birds were staking claims, getting ready to make nests. They were alive, also, with flashing movement, and for once, at this special time of year, the birds ignored Douglas and Angeline. A compulsion drove them harder in springtime than any other time; for a few weeks not even predators nor two-legged creatures, could quite divert them.

Douglas stood and watched. 'The time of awakening,' he said, in Sioux, and turned when she asked what he had said. 'Springtime; all the sleeping things are opening their eyes.'

She looked sombrely at the treetops where all that tumult was. 'I want to see your mountains,' she said softly. 'I've never been to the top, now or any other time of year. It must be beautiful up there now.'

It *was* beautiful, but that didn't describe it, not really, because the beauty was always there, even in mid-winter. This time of year Cade's mountain and the farther peaks and meadows showed the key of existence, the secret of life and the purpose of everything that moved on the surface of the waterways and through the forests, and that grazed the parks.

'Will you take me up there, Douglas?'

It required almost a full day just to reach the trail to the top. After that, it took another six-hour ride to reach the cabin. And that was only the beginning. To see the farther places, the virgin hinterlands, would take more days and nights. But he did not explain it that way. He said, 'Maybe. Someday,' and freed her hand to lean and steady the canoe while she stepped in. Only she did not step in.

'When?'

He looked around. She was rooted and her jaw was tough-set. He sighed, straightened up and turned around. 'You can't even reach the cabin in one day. Maybe, if your paw would like to go along sometime, or if you have some friend or something, we could—'

'Just us, Douglas.'

He gazed at her. 'Three, maybe four or five days back in the mountains alone?' He shook his head. 'Get in the canoe; I'm curious to see how we're going to buck the current all those miles back to town.'

She smiled at him and started past to the canoe, but on impulse she turned, and on impulse he reached for her. The banked fires of winter were no longer smouldering, not in the trees, not among the birds, and not with the man and the girl. He kissed her with a bruising want and she met his passion with one that equalled it.

Then she hung breathless in his arms and pushed her cheek against his chest, face averted. He felt the solid pound of each heartbeat, felt the pressure of her his full length, and was mindful of nothing but this.

She said, 'I'm not ashamed. Are you?'

He wasn't. It never would have occurred to him to be ashamed. But he *was* emotionally off-balance; it was hard to think rationally. 'Not ashamed,' he told her. 'Something else, but I don't know what it is . . . I wanted to do this that first day up at the meadow.'

She said, 'I understand.' She locked both hands behind him and squeezed. He was surprised again, at her strength. 'I don't know how it could happen like this, Douglas. It—one minute it wasn't—the next minute it was.'

He said, in a wondering voice, 'I love you. I think about you all the time. I see you when I close my eyes.' Then he said something that made her finally move back and look up. 'I wonder if we need the same things and if we'll turn out to share thoughts?'

'Share thoughts?'

'Cade said a man and a woman have to share thoughts and needs. Otherwise when hibernation is over, they go away separately.'

She loosened her hold and reached to push back a thick coil of hair. 'We just now shared them, Douglas. I did not mean to kiss you. I don't think you meant to kiss me. It just came out of both of us. Is that a shared thought?'

He loosened and looked down into her lifted face.

'You see how large that sky is? Well, I have a feeling for you that is even bigger.' He smiled. 'I'll tell you—I've never been in love with a girl before.'

She smiled back. *'I'll* tell *you* something: You had never better love another one.'

He put his palm to her smooth cheek. It was like warm velvet. He took the hand away and let out a shaky big breath. Then he pulled himself around and bent to steady the canoe again. 'Get in.'

She did not move this time either. 'When will you take me to your mountains?'

'Get in and don't tempt me. I would take you there today, or tomorrow, and I'd never bring you back.' As she stepped past into the canoe, lightly and with perfect balance, he raised up to also step in. 'I feel like everything inside me is tied in a knot.' He did not look at her, but eased down carefully, picked up a paddle and pushed the canoe backwards into the shoals. 'What do you feel like, Angeline?'

She laughed a little when she answered. 'Like I've never felt before, Douglas. Like I'll die if you go away. Like all the beauty in the world is flowing over this canoe, and nothing like this can ever happen to anyone else. Like it must go on and on and on. I've been waiting for you for a long time.'

They did not talk any more for an hour. Paddling against even the weaker current of the shallows was hard work. He kept at it with powerful strokes because he needed something like this, needed some kind of physical release. He wanted to plunge the paddle to the river-bottom and propel them forward by mighty heaves and strains. He wanted to be exhausted.

Against this kind of resolve they made excellent time, and by the mid-afternoon were back in the broader, less forceful stretch of river just below North Fork. Not even a springtime river's swollen force could stand against that furious compulsion that made Douglas wear himself out getting them back.

They paused to rest a mile below town in a little back-bay where the water pooled in a sluggish circular ripple. He was exhausted and leaned on the paddle looking back. Angeline leaned and said, 'We can leave the canoe here and walk the rest of the way. You haven't rested in three miles.'

He might have agreed except that if they left her canoe here, below town, if someone did not steal it someone would still have to eventually paddle it the rest of the way. He shook his head, dipped the paddle to shoot them out of the backwater, and together they made the last mile in very good time.

Then they tied the canoe, threw the same camou-flaging bush-tops over it she had had it covered with before, and sank down upon the warm, sloping river-bank to lie a long time and rest. Here, they talked again. Here too, Douglas finally resolved the smouldering con-tradictions within him. He would learn to live with them because he had to. As best he could, he would control and restrain them.

As best he could.

When Angeline raised up on one arm and tickled his neck with a weed-stalk, he twisted over to look upwards. She was less than arm's length distant. She was voluptuous and beautiful, she was passionate and a full woman in every way. Restraint was hard. As he lay looking at her he thought it was only going to get harder.

'Your father would shoot me,' he murmured.

She dropped the weed-stalk. 'My father already knows.'

Douglas stared. 'How can that be?'

'Simple,' she said. 'I told him. Douglas, a woman knows before a man does. Ordinarily, anyway. If you hadn't kissed me today. If you hadn't said—what you said—I'd have said it to you. I'm in love with you. I've been in love with you for a week—but it seems like a whole lifetime.' She reared back when he shifted position to free his arms. 'Not here, right in town.' She sprang up and looked down with her lips curled and teasing. 'Walk me home. I need a guide because I can't see anything but star-bursts.'

He got up and moved easily at her side. He remembered, several days back when he'd gone to the *Emporium,* her father had seemed different towards him. He remembered that, but he had made no attempt, then, to understand it.

He did not think he understood it now, when he looked at her; what father of such a girl wouldn't feel his soul shrivelling at the prospect of losing her—even to a young man with promise. What must her father feel now, if he knew she was in love with a man who had nothing, who at least did not have very *much,* and who was not really trained for any trade that would enable him to support a wife?

By the time they reached her house on Elm Street, and he was up on the porch with her, it was beginning to dawn on him that he had no business doing what he had done. He had no business doing anything like this at all.

TWELVE

NORTH FORK'S POSSEMEN

Stuart Campbell was like most men who never married, who made their way alone through life; he was neither addicted to excessive bathing nor to excessive patience. When Gabriel Longstreet came to the shop the third day after Douglas Weldon had learned about paddling a canoe, and complained that when he tried to talk to young Weldon over at Clancy's place, Weldon had not only said nothing, he had got up in mid-sentence and had walked out on Longstreet.

The gunsmith was using pumice on a rifle-stock to achieve the perfection he demanded before applying the oil and wax. He kept right on working as he said, 'Well; folks have a bad habit of figuring that when *they* want to talk, so does the other feller. And maybe he don't.'

'He's been acting different for the past few days. Even Dick Ullman noticed it, Stuart.'

Campbell grunted. 'Ullman's no judge of nothing.'

Longstreet got exasperated. 'How about Johnathon Barlow?'

Campbell put the rifle-stock to his cheek to test for absolute smoothness. 'Johnathon noticed too, did he? All right, Gabe.' Campbell put the rifle-stock gently upon a small sandbag atop his big workbench, and looked across at his visitor. 'All right. He sits in here like a gutshot buffler, too, but it's none of my doings so I figure it's none of my business. Any more'n it's your business. What the hell you stewing about it for anyway? Might be a touch of the summer complaint. That's common enough this time of year. Maybe the lad needs some sulphur and molasses to thin down his winter-thickened blood. But that's none of your—or my—business either, is it?'

'Stuart, how long do you think it takes to ride from Colorado to Montana?'

Old Campbell looked at the rifle-stock, stroked it with a leathery palm. 'Is that what's bothering you? I reckon the lad'll be ready, when he has to be.'

Longstreet could get no more satisfaction from old Campbell than just that final statement, although he lingered to press his idea of Douglas Weldon attending a strategy meeting of the Town Council. Then Longstreet left, heading for the jailhouse to confer again with Marshal Barlow, and he had not been gone long before Douglas also visited the gun shop. Campbell looked at him, then offered the pumiced rifle-stock to be felt.

'How does that strike you?' he asked, and when Weldon examined the stock and handed it back saying, 'Almost as soft as a girl's cheek,' the old man gazed steadily at him for a moment of dawning suspicion before he put the stock aside and went hunting for his pipe and pouch. When he came back stuffing shag into the bowl, Douglas Weldon was seated on a tilted-back chair beyond the counter gazing impassively out the window and diagonally across the road in the direction of the *Emporium.*

Campbell followed Weldon's sighting, blew smoke, settled comfortably at the workbench and said, 'Are you giving any thought to the Bentons?'

Douglas shook his head without looking back at the old man. Campbell privately dwelt upon these things, and after an interval of quiet silence he took a long chance by saying, 'Boy; you'd better shake them cobwebs out of your head and start figuring your strategy. Angie'll be less than a memory if they kill you. And they're going to, by gawd, if they can.'

Douglas turned quickly, the question forming on his lips that his eyes were already asking. Campbell puffed and made a little gesture to ward off words. He removed the pipe and peered into it, tamped ash with a callused thumbpad, then held it low and smiled.

'It's fine with me, Douglas, I think the world of her. Always have. And her mother afore her. Always held Alex in high favour too. You'll be doing yourself right proud. But not if they kill you.'

Douglas said, 'They're not going to kill me. As for the other—I don't have the answer to it.'

'To what?'

'Hell. I couldn't take her up to the mountain to live, and I don't have any trade but hunting and trapping.'

'Town marshal's job pays fair, Douglas.'

'No. Even if Mister Barlow quit, I wouldn't have it. You're probably right about a feller living down here owing something to the town, to the community, but wrong or not I wasn't raised to kill just for the sake of killing.' Douglas kept looking across the counter at the older man. 'I don't even know how to shoe a horse or be a bar-tender.'

Campbell put the pipe aside. 'Them two occupations don't have a hell of a big future anyhow.' He smiled into the strained, tight face of the younger man. 'Maybe you're sort of putting the cart afore the horse, though, son. Maybe you'd ought to make plumb sure of Angie, first.'

'I have,' mumbled Douglas, and turned back to looking out the window.

Campbell was stopped cold. 'You have? You and her have spoke together—about things?'

'Yes.'

'Well I'll be switched,' exclaimed the old man. 'Congratulations.'

Dick Ullman was hastening up the roadway. Douglas watched this instead of heeding the gunsmith. Ullman was a large, heavy man. When his kind hurried there had to be a reason. He turned to peer through the window from outside, then swerved and came quickly into the shop. Campbell, who had not been paying attention to who was passing outside, looked at Ullman, looked at Ullman's expression, and said, mildly, 'Something wrong?'

The horse trader's reply came harshly. 'Yeah, I'd say something's wrong.' He paused and looked over where Weldon was seated. 'A cowboy from west of town a few miles who rides for the sickle outfit come in a little while ago to report that someone hit their horse-herd and run off southward with about thirty head of good saddle-stock; the animals they'd just finished shoeing and getting ready for the spring work.'

Stuart Campbell was flabbergasted. 'In broad daylight?'

'No. Well; just at dawn, they figure. Maybe an hour before full light.'

Douglas studied Ullman thoughtfully. 'It's almost noon. They've got a big head start, even driving thirty horses. Mister Ullman; if the cow outfit knew the horses were missing at daybreak, why is their rider just now reaching town?'

'They sent him back,' stated Ullman. 'They all went chasing horsethieves, and after a while when they seen they were going to overhaul them ten miles or so below town, they sent this cowboy back to ask us to send down a posse. He told Johnathon by their sign it looked like maybe there was about eight or ten of them. The sickle outfit only has six riders, and that includes the rider they sent back. He lit out southward again as soon as he'd brought the news. If they corner them outlaws they'll need every gun they can get.' Ullman kept looking at Weldon. 'I left word for my dayman to saddle your animal. Now I got to get up there and recruit Gabe and as many of his yardmen as he can spare. Be back at the barn in ten minutes.' Ullman turned and hurried out, turned left and went hastening in the direction of the stage company's office and wagon-lot.

Douglas eased his chair down and arose. 'Ten miles is a damned big head-start,' he said, moving towards the door. 'If they stay to the prairie, maybe we can reach 'em, but it won't be done in a day.'

Stuart Campbell nodded agreement. 'If you do overhaul 'em, boy, it'll be carbine work. Good luck.'

Douglas walked out and headed towards the trading barn. Already, there were a number of men down there, mounted and bristling with armament. Others were coming on the run from several directions. It looked as though the town posse was going to be large enough, with men to spare.

Ullman's hostler came forth with Douglas Weldon's horse, handed over the reins, and was immediately yelled at by some newcomer who was in a hurry for his animal.

The men were talking among themselves loudly and excitedly. Douglas watched, listened, decided it was going to be another ten minutes at the least before Ullman returned and the posse was ready to leave town, so he walked back as far as the jailhouse, leading his horse. There, he left the animal at the rack and walked inside. Johnathon Barlow was sitting up looking agitated. He seized upon Weldon's entry to make a slightly breathless enquiry. Douglas assured him the posse was forming, that it was large enough to stop a small army, and unless the horsethieves sprouted wings, the posse would overtake them, eventually. Then he said, 'Why would they do a thing like this in daylight, especially when they were going to drive southward across a prairie where the dust from that big a herd would be visible for twenty miles in all directions?'

Barlow had evidently been asked this before, or else he had wondered about it, and had manufactured his own plausible explanation, because he had an answer on the tip of his tongue.

'They didn't want to steal a herd in the dark, and go

to all the work and risk, then discover by daylight they'd got someone's brood mares, or someone's old retired animals. They probably know exactly where they can get top dollar for well-broke, topnotch working stock horses. They needed light to make sure what they was getting.' Barlow swore. 'And dust or no dust, they're going to make it unless that damned posse gets to riding.'

Douglas agreed, at least with Barlow's last observation. 'I'll go stir 'em up and get 'em moving. If that cowboy who talked to you had waited a bit we'd have had a guide.'

'He had to get back. Those are pretty bad odds, you know. The sickle outfit's going to need every man it's got.' Barlow smiled crookedly. 'You can cut the sign, Douglas. Thirty horses and a bunch of riders behind them ought to leave a trail big enough for a blind man to be able to smell the dust and never have to look down.'

Douglas left, took his horse from the rack and started back where what looked like about twenty or twenty-five men were finally mounting up. Ullman was growling orders, as though he would lead. Douglas Weldon stepped astride his horse, eased in with the others, and when Ullman gestured overhead with a clenched fist, Douglas was swept along with the others.

It was afternoon, the weather was ideal, morale was high among the riders, and Douglas Weldon kept waiting for the horse trader to leave the stageroad somewhere southward and sashay back and forth until he picked up the horsethieves' trail. Ullman remained on the road.

When it seemed to Douglas they might pass the trail he loped ahead and told Ullman his thoughts. The trader said, 'They got to cross the road somewhere down here. When we find that place there'll be plenty of sign, then we'll go after them.'

Douglas did not argue. This was Ullman's posse. But he left it and coursed the wide prairie to the west. In fact he rode so far west he almost lost sight of the others, and he came upon no wide segment of churned earth of the kind thirty loose horses and ten ridden horses, all shod, would make. In fact, he didn't find any trail of horses at all, so he set his course on an angle, and eventually rejoined the posse about eight miles south of North Fork.

Ullman scowled when Douglas reported. 'They crossed back up-country somewhere, then,' he contended. 'And we just didn't see the sign.'

Douglas shook his head. 'No they didn't. We'd have seen the sign.'

The possemen clustered close, listening. Ullman was perspiring. He was also beginning to get irritated. 'Well, they sure as hell didn't *fly* over. They made better time than we figured; we'll find their tracks crossing the road down-country another few miles.'

Douglas did not dispute this. He was deliberately avoiding an argument; at least he was trying to avoid one.

But riding further down the road was only going to make matters worse, so he said, 'Maybe if we split up and scouted on both sides of the road, Mister Ullman . . .'

The crowding-up horsemen seemed to approve of this, but Dick Ullman's face reddened. He narrowed his eyes at Weldon. 'If we split up, and a handful of us find them outlaws, your idea could get some men killed. Have you figured that?'

Douglas checked a hot retort, let a moment pass, then said, 'I'll tell you one thing, Mister Ullman, and you can make out of it anything you want. There didn't any thirty loose horses being herded by ten mounted men cross this road anywhere behind us and I'll bet my life on it.'

'West then,' someone said.

Douglas shook his head. 'Not west. I sashayed all over that country. Didn't any forty shod animals go down-country in that direction either.'

Even Dick Ullman would not question Douglas Weldon's ability to read the sign, so Dick and all the others sat there looking at Douglas. Finally Dick said, 'You got an idea?'

Douglas had, but it had not made much sense, even to him, when he first considered it. 'Someone's a damned liar. If some cow outfit lost its horse-herd to outlaws, he lied when he rode to town to get a posse to go chasing *southward.*'

THIRTEEN

THE ARRIVAL OF DISASTER

For a long while no one said anything. The implication behind Weldon's words took a little time to get used to. If the horsethieves had not run southward, then why had that sickle rider said they had? If Weldon was sure there were no tracks . . .

A man with a nasal voice suddenly swore. 'Gawddammit—it just come to me: Sickle's a small outfit. *Six* riders. Since when do *six* riders use *thirty* horses?'

Ullman sat humped in the saddle looking baffled and troubled and angry. But he was not ready to admit he had been fooled; he would not admit it to himself, let alone to twenty other men. 'Counting teams and all,' he mumbled, 'thirty horses might be right.'

Weldon was not concerned with the number of horses, he was concerned with the plain fact that no big band of horses had come southward, voluntarily or under the urging of riders.

'That cowboy who rode into town,' he said to Ullman. 'Did you know him?'

Ullman hadn't, but that was plausible. 'This time of year with the ranches hiring on, one cowboy is just like another one to us folks in town. We don't get to know most of them until about mid-summer when they've been around a while.'

Douglas made his decision. 'I'm going back. You can keep hunting sign if you want to.' He turned his horse, and Ullman growled at him.

'Whatever's going on ain't in town, Weldon.'

Douglas threw his answer over one shoulder and kept right on riding. 'You want to bet money on that? Why else did that cowboy want a posse raised in North Fork, then sent charging down here?' He booted his horse over into a lope and did not look back.

The men with Dick Ullman were of two minds. Some, reluctant to change, now that they were so far down-country, and still clinging to a furry hope that there *were* outlaws just ahead, sat humped and unmoving. A number of other men, already transferring their loyalty from Ullman to Weldon, turned without more talk and urged their horses back the way they had come.

Later, they all did this, but by then Douglas Weldon was two miles north and still riding. He did not know, and did not especially care, whether everyone returned with him or not.

The night was turning chilly, but there was a big moon, not quite full but amply large to brighten the gloom, and the sky was cloudless, so there were also thousands of diamond-bright stars to help visibility, except that there was nothing to see, as Douglas rode back.

He began to form an idea. It was vague and improbable, with nothing really to support it, but otherwise he could not account for the ruse that had emptied North Fork of so many armed men. But he did not mention it, when the riders finally caught up and talked as they rode. There was no point in causing consternation now; when they reached town they would learn soon enough, if the idea was right or wrong.

Ullman was the last rider to reach the main body on its return, and he kept entirely to himself. Something like this could be especially hard on a man who could not accept the possibility of personal fallibility. The others left him alone, and that did not help much, either. Whenever they sought an answer, they called their questions to Douglas Weldon. Dick Ullman, who had led his big posse out of town with a clenched fist, was now trailing it back again in humiliation.

They saw the lights while still a long way out. It was not actually very late, only about eight o'clock, but even so North Fork usually began bedding down by eight, and now it seemed that most of the homes and stores had their lamps lit. That was enough to cause a ripple of worried conversation among the possemen.

When they reached the lower end of town it was obvious something was seriously wrong. The first person to accost them, as they entered town riding at a walk, riding all bunched up and observant, was a thick, coarse woman who lived at that end of town but who had a bakery shop up nearer the centre of the business district. She was crossing the road hugging a shapeless old sweater against the cold, and saw the horsemen coming. She stopped dead-still in the roadway until she recognized some of them, then she said, 'Too late. You're an hour too late. They already been here and gone. And they took Alex and Gabe and Angie with 'em.'

The possemen stopped, dumbstruck. All but one. Douglas Weldon walked his horse right on past the woman to the rack out front of the jailhouse, stepped down in a blaze of light as someone opened the door, dismounted and brushed past a man in a heavy coat who said something to him, and entered. The outer office was full of men, all talking at the same time. They recognized Weldon, who shouldered through without speaking and went back where another clutch of noisily agitated men were in Johnathon Barlow's cell. The marshal was white, and trying, with the help of two men, to sit up, to swing his legs over the side of the bunk.

Douglas put a hand upon Barlow's chest and held steady. To the men who were on either side he said, 'Let go. Leave him alone.' They obeyed. Men, crowding in from the front office helped to fill the little cell-room to overflowing. It was deathly quiet as Barlow raised his contorted face. Sweat stood on his forehead and upper lip. Douglas slowly wagged his head. 'Lie back, Marshal.'

'I can't. I got to—'

Douglas leaned a little weight against the weaker man, forcing him to obey. 'Lie back. Quit worrying. There are enough men without you.'

Barlow had to yield. He was too weak not to. But he did not yield until the pressure compelled him to, then he lay back and someone picked up his legs and arranged them, too.

Barlow's expression was terrible. 'You know what happened, Douglas?'

'Some woman told us at the lower end of town.'

Barlow gasped from his recent exertion. 'There was four of them. The one who rode in earlier saying he was a sickle rider . . .'

'Yeah, I know. That was one of them.' Douglas looked into the shadowy crowd of faces. 'Anyone got a pony of whiskey?' Someone handed him a small bottle and he removed the cap, put it into Barlow's hand and said, 'Drink, Marshal.'

Barlow obeyed, afterwards handed back the bottle, and panted for a moment, but good colour flushed his face. He settled a calmer look upon Weldon. 'You know who it was?'

Douglas knew. 'The Bentons?'

Barlow nodded, while behind Weldon a low sound of assent came from the crowd. Barlow said, 'They never figured to ride in and challenge you in a gunfight, Douglas. In trouble like this it don't happen that way.'

Douglas had no difficulty believing this. He had been hearing tales of hostages since he'd been a child. 'How many?'

'Four. Two Bentons, and a couple of others.' Barlow needed a shave, when he ran a hand over his face it made a distinct, scratchy sound.

'When they left town, which way did they ride?' Douglas asked, and Barlow exchanged a look with Clancy before answering, a cautious look.

'They left word, Douglas, before they rode out, that they'd trade one hostage for one man. They want the fellers who killed Charley Benton that night up the pass.'

'But those men are gone,' said Weldon. 'They've been gone a week or more.'

Clancy spoke up. 'Sure, but the Bentons won't accept that. They want a man for a hostage, otherwise they told us they would send 'em back, Angeline, Alex, and Gabe, one at a time, tied face down across their horses, dead.' Clancy looked stonily at Douglas Weldon. 'They rode north towards the foothills. That's where they'll hole-up. But there's all those flat miles between, Douglas. They'd see a posse coming long before it got across the prairie. They'd start killing hostages.'

Clancy, Barlow, all the others who were standing inside the jailhouse, seemed to be placing the responsibility on Douglas Weldon, as though he were not only the instigator of the Charley Benton killing, but also as though he were either at fault for the present situation, or the salvation of it. The basis for this feeling was basic enough; whether his companions that night in the pass had fled or not, he had been the leader, he was still in North Fork, and whatever came of the present situation, he was going to be blamed for it.

Barlow said, 'If you ride up there, you got to go alone, and if you do that, they're going to kill you sure as gawd made green apples—and we can't count on them keeping their word about releasing the hostages even then, because they don't believe them other three men have disappeared. We're between hell and a hot place. Ordinarily we could maybe raise three volunteers, but not this time. No man wants to leave town like they say, knowing damned well he's going to get killed without a lousy chance.'

There was a brief interruption out front when an hysterical woman came to the door. Some of the townsmen took her away talking loudly in a soothing way. She was Belinda, the wife of Gabe Longstreet.

Douglas arose without saying any more and stalked through the crowd towards the roadway. No one got in his way, and when a couple of townsmen murmured Clancy shut them up. 'Leave the lad be. He needs time.'

'We ain't got a whole lot,' exclaimed a gravelly voice from the mob of men turning to leave the cell-room for the outer office.

Clancy waited until he was left alone with Marshal

Barlow, then he pulled up a bench and sighed as he dropped downward. 'They'll kill 'em sure as hell,' he stated bluntly. 'If the lad goes up there come morning, they'll kill him too.'

The reasoning behind Clancy's statement was simple, and Barlow knew what it was. 'How in the hell are you going to get anyone to ride out behind the lad? We don't have three men in the country who are that tired of living, Mike.'

'Damned awful spot to be in,' mumbled Clancy. 'I wish to hell they'd take money instead.'

Barlow did not even offer a comment about that; they *wouldn't* take money, so why talk about it? Out front, the sound of voices sounded strong. Barlow said, 'You better get some help, Mike, and make damned sure some well-meaning soul doesn't try to get up a posse and go charging up there.'

Clancy nodded but made no move to depart. He sat glumly on the bench, hunched forward, hands clasped. Finally he spoke as though the worst had already happened. 'We'd ought to be ready to go after them, though, Johnathon. I'd guess they'll be finished before noon tomorrow.'

That was probably true, but as Barlow said, any sign of resistance from town would hasten the massacre. 'They'll be watching down this way like hawks. They probably got a spy-glass. Any sign that we're getting ready, Mike, and it'll end a lot quicker. We got until noon.'

Clancy looked up. 'To do what?'

Barlow did not answer because he had no answer.

Clancy went back to studying his clasped hands. 'We could use the telegraph and get the army over the mountains to send down a company to cut them off from behind, from the top of the pass.' Clancy threw up his hands. 'But that ain't the problem, is it? Because by the time the army could get there, they'd have killed our people. What the hell do we do, Johnathon?'

It was a question everyone had been asking now for several hours and no one had yet come up with an answer. Marshal Barlow grudgingly shook his head. 'Think,' he said, 'Think of something, Gawddammit, *I* don't know.'

Clancy arose to depart, at the cell door he turned and said, 'I'll talk to young Weldon.'

Barlow nodded about that but without showing any hope, any encouragement, and after Clancy walked out, gently closing the cell-room door after himself, Marshal Barlow groaned and let his head fall back in defeat. There was no way, no way at all, as long as the Bentons would not believe those three cowboys who had gone with Weldon that night, were long gone. But even if they had still been in North Fork it was very improbable that they would have ridden northward, one at a time.

The jailhouse was warm, as opposed to the nightly chill outside. Before the men out there went solemnly trooping up to the Montana House behind Mike Clancy, someone had the presence of mind to stoke the stove.

There were a lot of stoked-stoves that night in North Fork. Everyone knew what had happened, and knew the impossible dilemma the Benton brothers' ultimatum had created. The men in town despaired of the lives of Longstreet and Farraday, and, along with the women, they also despaired of the life of Angeline.

FOURTEEN

THREE UNLIKELY NIGHTRIDERS

A man whose formative years had been spent according to the laws of nature, inherently thought in those terms. Douglas Weldon went down to the gun shop and found Stuart Campbell having tea and fried bread in his living quarters out back. The old man did not seem surprised when he shuffled up front and unlocked the door for his visitor. He did not seem surprised the way things had turned out in town, either, although that came out only gradually, after he had taken Douglas out back where Campbell had bread frying.

He offered to share his supper. Douglas declined. He offered tea and Douglas declined that too. Tinned tea was a luxury; the kind he and Old Cade had shared on the mountain had been made from sassafrass and foxberry leaves.

Old Campbell finished frying his bread, put it on a plate, poured molasses over it and sat down to eat. He said, 'You know the whole story by now,' and filled his mouth, having offered openers to the conversation.

Douglas answered by asking a question. 'Who are the two best shots in North Fork?'

Campbell chewed in slow rhythm as he pondered his answer. 'Aren't too many,' he eventually answered. 'That's one thing rapid-fire weapons do—make real marksmanship unnecessary. I'd say maybe Peter Given and Dick Ullman.' Campbell loaded his mouth again and watched his visitor's face. When he swallowed and could speak again, he said, 'You know that if you try what you're thinkin', and it fails, you'd better not return to North Fork, don't you?'

Douglas knew that. He also knew that doing nothing was going to eventually result in the same thing; people held him responsible for Charley Benton's killing whether he had done it or not. They held him responsible for the other Bentons being in the country. Give them a little time to settle upon a scapegoat, and he, being the only one still around who had been connected to that earlier affair, was going to be blamed for everything.

Instead of involving either of them in this kind of discussion, though, he said, 'Who is Peter Given?'

Campbell grinned. 'Preacher.' At the look he got, old Campbell's grin broadened. 'For a fact. He's the Presbyterian preacher. But don't let that scare you off. Him and

God got a good understanding.'

'Would he shoot a man?'

Campbell had to worry that one around a bit before answering it. 'He could answer that a lot better'n I could. I reckon he would—if he had to. Like I just said, him and God got a good understanding—of how things *are,* not how him and God figure they ought to be.' Campbell looked around for his cup, picked it up, drank tea, then put it down. 'You ever met him?'

Douglas hadn't. 'No. Can you get him to the shop tonight?'

Stuart Campbell sighed. 'I reckon. You figure the three of you can do it?'

Douglas looked old Campbell squarely in the eye. 'Who else can?'

Campbell said, 'No one. You got until daybreak.' He examined a broken fingernail. 'Ullman will be your biggest problem. He's a natural-born overbearing out-sized bastard.'

Douglas had never doubted this for one moment. If there had been almost any alternative he'd have chosen it. 'But he's a true shot?'

Campbell pushed his plate and cup aside and got stiffly to his feet. 'Maybe even better'n the preacher. I've seen him shoot. When will you be back?'

Douglas also arose. 'As soon as I can bring Ullman.'

They went back out through the darkened shop and Weldon stepped outside. He saw men standing in small clusters here and there on both sides of the road as he headed for the trading barn. When people looked at him he did not look back. Marshal Barlow and others would never agree to what he had in mind. Old Campbell would, but that was simply because the gunsmith belonged to another time; human life—*any* life—had not been so valuable then, and desperate means had, in those earlier times, been commonplace.

Dick Ullman was alone in his cubbyhole office when Douglas walked in. Ullman was smoking a foul cigar which he put aside when he recognized his caller, his tawny, small eyes showing dark malevolence. Douglas gave Ullman no chance; there was reason for the trader to feel antagonistic, particularly after the fiasco he had led earlier, but Douglas was not concerned with that.

'I need two marksmen,' he told the trader. 'Mostly, I need a couple of men who can keep their mouths closed. I was told you're one of the best shots around.'

Ullman slowly put the cigar back between his teeth and clamped down on it, hard. 'For what?' he growled.

'Three men can get into the mountains before daylight.'

Ullman stared and said nothing.

'Any more men will make noise or get in the way,' went on Douglas. 'And for this job they've got to be the best shots in North Fork.'

Ullman still said nothing. He chewed the cigar and continued to look evil.

'We've got to leave town by the back way so Barlow or Clancy, or someone else, won't know we're going. We've got to get into the mountains, far back, before dawn.'

Ullman flung the cigar into a brass cuspidor. 'Then what?'

Douglas did not know; at least he was not sure. 'It'll depend on where they are when we find them.'

'But you're figuring on long-range marksmanship, aren't you?' asked the big, burly man.

'Maybe. If it comes to that. Otherwise, I'm figuring on something safer. Do you have any whiskey around here?'

Ullman's tufted brows climbed. 'Yes, a couple quarts. You got some silly idea of getting them renegades drunk?'

'How about laudanum; you got some of that among your doctoring medicines?'

Now, Ullman lost his cold look of plain antagonism. 'Laudanum? You out of your mind?'

'Do you have any?'

'Sure. But what the hell good is—'

'We're going to half fill one quart of your whiskey with the laudanum, and we're not going to doctor the other bottle.'

Understanding came slowly to Dick Ullman, but it came. 'All right. But I'll tell you what I think: Anyone who rides in on them fellers is going to get shot out of hand. They aren't going to fall for any tricks like—'

'But if I get shot,' said Douglas, breaking in sharply, 'it's still a good gamble that four men who've spent a cold night and a cold morning, will want a pull off a whiskey bottle, isn't it?'

Ullman slumped back in his chair gazing at the younger man. 'I reckon. Then why not doctor both bottles?'

'Because I'm going to ride down into their camp drinking out of one.' Douglas leaned on the grimy wall and studied Ullman. 'Will you come along?'

Ullman pondered, and by whatever devious chain of reasoning he arrived at the decision, he nodded his head. 'I reckon so. When?'

'Just as soon as you fetch the bottles and the laudanum, to be doctored right here, right now, then we're going back up the road to Campbell's shop. That's where we'll pick up the preacher.'

Ullman blinked. 'Preacher?'

'Reverend Given. He's the next best marksman isn't he?'

Ullman pitched himself up out of his chair with a loud protest. 'Gawd a'mighty, Weldon, you can't expect a feller like Pete Given to snipe somebody.'

Douglas shot his reply right back. 'Who else, then? There are four outlaws, up there, Mister Ullman, and I don't give a damn how good you are with a rifle—if I'm down there with them when the trouble comes, you aren't going to be able to get more than one before they get me. But if there are *two* sharpshooters hidden up in the forest, you and this preacher—and me in their camp, also armed and ready—*three* good shots can down four average ones any day in the year. But if I don't make it, and if the doctored whiskey doesn't work, then there are still the two of you, and at least you'll be able to get out of there alive.'

Ullman listened intently. When Douglas finished he pursed his lips and went to a cupboard, rummaged a moment among the containers of liniment, healing oils and salves, brought forth a purple bottle which he set aside, then ducked down and groped in a desk drawer for the two quart bottles of whiskey. Until he was working the caps loose he said nothing, but as he measured out the whiskey and measured in the laudanum, he said, 'Don't get the wrong bottle. This stuff'll knock you out harder'n being mule-kicked in the head.'

Fifteen minutes later they left for the gun shop. But they trudged up the dark and empty back alley all the way, and emerged upon the front roadway only when it was necessary, out front of Campbell's place.

Stuart still had not lighted a lamp in the front of his shop, but he'd left a rear door open and that permitted some light to filter through.

The Reverend Peter Given was a tall, thin man with a prominent Adams-apple. He had a shock of unruly curly hair and a wide, thin mouth. His nod, like his stare, was cautious. Campbell had already explained the basic idea to him, and Reverend Given had not committed himself, yes or no, but when Douglas explained about the doctored whiskey, Peter Given smiled and approved.

'I'll go,' he exclaimed. 'If we don't accomplish anything else, gentlemen, we'll have demonstrated the evils of the Demon Rum.'

Ullman said, 'Whiskey, not rum,' and turned to Stuart Campbell. 'I'd like to borrow that Kentucky rifle of yours, if you got no objection.'

Stuart pointed. On his workbench three long-barrelled rifles were lying one above the other. The topmost rifle was Old Cade's gun. That was for Douglas.

The Reverend Peter Given was a new kind of individual to Douglas. He understood perfectly how churchmen felt about taking life; to a great extent he agreed perfectly with it. But not in this situation, and he had to know what the minister's thoughts were. But he hesitated; Reverend Given was an unknown quotient. With anyone else Douglas would have asked his question straight out. Now, he looked at the tall, thin man, and hung fire.

Stuart Campbell guessed the trouble. 'Reverend Pete,' he said, 'how does your conscience set on justifiable killing?'

Given did not even hesitate. 'On *justifiable* killing, my conscience rests plumb easy.' He looked from Campbell to Douglas. Behind them, Dick Ullman was handling the Kentucky rifle, getting the feel. Given smiled. 'Mister Weldon, tonight I figure the three of us will be instruments of the Lord. And, Mister Weldon, if we don't light out of here plumb soon, we're never going to be in the mountains before first-light, are we?'

It took fifteen minutes for Ullman to saddle his horse, a mount for Peter Given, and rig out Weldon's animal. During that short interlude Douglas hastened to his room at the hotel, changed his clothing, kept only the quick-draw holster and the short-barrelled sixgun from his former dress, and slipped out the back way heading for the trading barn dressed in the same old blanket-coat and smoke-tanned moccasins he'd worn on his first appearance in town the previous month.

The town was still full of restless men and women, but they were around front, not in the alleyway where Dick Ullman handed the reins around. In moonlight Ullman looked almost happy, almost pleased, about something. Douglas noticed, but did not make any issue of this. They still had to get away from town without rousing people.

Ullman led the way, due west across littered empty lots and around stables, cow-sheds and chicken houses. Some dogs came forth to stand stiff-legged and bark, but as far as Douglas could see, no one saw them. At least no one came out of any of the residences they passed, and made a point of staring at them.

Beyond town, Douglas called to Ullman, and this was something that Stuart Campbell would have understood:

There could not be *two* leaders. Douglas did not try tact, because he knew he was not experienced in it. But more than that, he wanted the understanding to be clear on both sides.

'You stay back,' he told Ullman. 'If there's need for any of us to ride off alone, I'll tell you when and where.'

Reverend Given looked down his thin nose at Ullman. Evidently he knew Dick's temper too.

Ullman reined down and let Douglas come up even with him. 'You're the mountain man, I'm not,' he said.

Their flint-on-steel relationship, up to this time, was resolved that easily and that quickly.

Douglas rode ahead a few yards. Behind him Given and Ullman rode side-by-side in almost stoic silence. There was a very good chance none of them would ride back, and there was an equally as good a chance that what they were doing was going to result in three people being murdered. Under those circumstances conversation, even relevant conversation, did not appeal to them.

FIFTEEN

INTO THE MOUNTAINS

It was close to midnight and although the chill did not penetrate because the men were dressed for it, it was there, noticeable in their steamy breath.

That same lop-sided old moon was above that had

brightened the prairie hours back when Douglas Weldon had gone quartering for the sign of thirty stolen horses, only now it was farther above in the centre of its firmament, and its light seemed more diffused, more ghostly and subject to shadows.

Douglas guessed that the Bentons had done as those other strangers to the North Fork country had done; headed up the stageroad. Except that he knew the Bentons would have gone off to one side or the other, to the east or the west, to make their camp, their site for the dawnlight vigil, which the previous outlaws had not done because their objective had been different.

Accordingly, Douglas led Ullman and Given more to the west. Several miles more westerly, in fact, and when Ullman said he did not think it was necessary to throw in that extra mile, Douglas was patient.

'We're not going to run any risks if we don't have to. They don't have to see us, Mister Ullman. All they have to do is *hear* us. Noise travels a long way on a clear night.'

That was all the talk until, just short of the broken, tilted country up ahead, something resembling a loose horse gave them a bad moment. It turned out to be a night-feeding cow elk. Reverend Given called the elk a name, but in a tone of voice that was soft and gentle. Douglas smiled in the darkness.

They had no trouble navigating the brakes even though moonlight and starshine were as often as not blocked out by thick upthrusts of pure stone. Douglas knew all this country. He led the way down through a narrow pass between sandstone barrancas, and back up out again where the trees were arrayed in company-front, as though to discourage invaders to the rearward forest.

They halted for a brief rest when it was no longer possible for them to be seen. Here, in quiet council, Dick Ullman advanced the theory that the Bentons had to be a mile or more to the west; somewhere, he thought, above but near, the stageroad. The minister thought this was probable, and turned for verification to Douglas Weldon. As far as Douglas was concerned, the exact location of the outlaws was not as yet critical enough for them to worry about it.

That the Bentons would be to the west, he had never doubted from the moment they left town, but whether that meant west of the roadway, or just to the west of where Douglas now was, with his companions, was worth considering—*only* after he and the others got far above, northward, where they could then come down-country, hopefully behind the outlaw-camp. He led off angling slightly westward, but more directly northward.

There were game-trails everywhere, by the score. The secret of the mountains was knowing which trail to take. Douglas knew them better than he knew the back-streets of North Fork.

He led Ullman and Given to a grassy plateau, and on

across that to an aspen patch where white-barked trees made tinkling sounds with their pale, round little leaves, when the faintest breeze came along. From the aspen grove he dipped to the dark depths of a canyon that was wooded with stubby, very old oaks, and here their horses reacted to the strong scent of bear by willingly climbing back up out without the customary unwillingness.

Reverend Given rode it all, the bad places and the good places, without a murmur. Douglas, looking back occasionally, began to suspect that this was not Given's first trip into the back country, although he could imagine no reason why a preacher of the gospel would feel called upon to go where there were no people, neither white ones nor red ones.

When they halted again, they had climbed considerably, but almost never by a direct route. Game-trails invariably followed *around* mountains, not straight up them. The horses were ready for a rest, so Douglas dismounted, Cade's old rifle cradled in one arm, and faced southward.

The distant prairie looked pewter. Where North Fork was nothing showed, unless it was a tiny smudge, a tiny spot of vague darkness that could be nothing more than a cloud-shadow, except that there were no clouds.

Lower, the landforms were uneven, watershed canyons meeting in deep swales where darkness puddled, where rims and crooked ridgetops meandered indifferently to the farthest higher country.

What Douglas had hoped to see was not down there:
A little fire.

Reverend Given came up and squatted, his cadaverous frame scarcely casting a shadow. He said, 'How is it that a reasoning animal can be here, as we are tonight, seeing all that soft, moonlighted grandeur, and still doubt a Creator exists?'

Ullman came up and sank to one knee, also plumbing the lower elevations for firelight. Neither he nor Douglas answered Reverend Given.

Ullman, who had never been this far back in the mountains before, leaned like a bear, looking in all directions, but mostly back down where they had been. It was possible, by moonlight, to see the pale run of the stageroad below and to their left. It was also possible, by twisting half around, to see the black-rock cliffs up where Charley Benton had died.

Douglas pointed. 'They will be down there somewhere, probably to the east.'

'Without a light,' said Ullman, 'it's going to be damned hard.'

Reverend Given caught Ullman's attention. 'There will be a light. We just happen to have too many treetops between us and it.' He scanned the eastward country. 'Over there, I'd guess, gentlemen. Somewhere not too far off the stageroad.'

Douglas agreed and stood up to lean with both hands upon Cade's rifle. 'We'll have to scout most of that country on foot, and even then there's no promise their horses won't scent us and nicker. But at least our horses won't answer back. Let's go.'

They went back, got astride, and almost at once Douglas's course tipped down towards the easterly watersheds. He kept the ghostly roadway in front of him, and when it was clearer, he searched round for a swale, and dismounted to tie his horse there without a word. Given and Ullman did the same. Given also swept back his long coat and tucked it tidily under a well-worn shell-belt. Ullman and Douglas exchanged a look; Ullman almost smiled.

Moving out on foot, now, the cold was less noticeable, but the hush was much deeper and that called for caution. Douglas never walked noisily, even in his boots, but Ullman and Peter Given rattled over pinecones, snapped twigs, even dislodged hidden little rocks, until Douglas called a halt and said, 'Listen you two, I'd just as soon not telegraph our coming a half-hour ahead. Damn it, look where you step!'

After that the noise grew less, but neither Ullman nor Given ever really mastered the ability to walk soundlessly, which was remarkable to Douglas, because they were in a forest, with six inches of spongy, sound-absorbing pine and fir needles underfoot.

They passed the place where Charley Benton had died. Douglas said nothing. They also passed a cougar-killed buck deer, with the blood still dripping, so evidently their scent had frightened off the big cat, but Ullman kept his rifle in both hands as they passed this spot. Undoubtedly, the panther was not very far away. Perhaps he was stalking the men, watching, to be sure they did not molest his fresh kill.

The road was very close now, and within another mile they would be in the same territory Douglas was certain the outlaws were using. He felt for the whiskey bottles, one in each coat pocket. Given saw him do this and closed the separating distance in three gangling strides.

'We should stop around here somewhere and wait for better light,' he said to Douglas. 'No one can accurately use a gun in darkness.'

Douglas agreed, smiled, and kept right on going.

Finally, he saw the orange movement, the bright, tiny flicker of firelight. An upraised arm halted the others. They could also see it. Ullman said in a growly whisper it looked less than a half mile below and slightly to their right, further from the roadway but well in sight of it.

Reverend Given was already thinking ahead. 'Satan's minions rest before returning to the Pit.'

Ullman looked up, then looked away again. Ordinarily, when he disagreed, he spoke out. So far he had not once argued with the minister. Douglas noticed that, without attaching more than passing significance to it. He took them on down another quarter mile, then a full half mile, and eventually he halted when the smoke-fragrance reached to where they were. This was close enough. He searched out a comfortable place and leaning Cade's rifle upon a tree, sat cross-legged at its base. Ullman kept his gun in hand. Reverend Given leaned upon his weapon looking more stork-like than ever. 'First-light will be along in about an hour,' he said, and smiled at Ullman's sceptical look. 'No man is born to the ministry, Mister Ullman. They are *called* to it. I was not called until fairly late in my early life, and prior to heeding the illumination, I was a cowboy. I was also a dealer in gambling rooms. And I was also a man in whom the wickedness of original sin lay like a black stain.'

Dick said, 'Uh huh, Reverend,' in a voice plainly meant to be placating.

'I robbed stages,' said Given, smiling sweetly down into Ullman's shocked face, 'and I rode the back trails through country like this—so when I say it's about an hour to first-light you can take my word for it. I learned a lot of things when I was on the run, Mister Ullman, besides a fast draw and rifle marksmanship.'

Ullman's face made Douglas want to laugh, but he didn't. Reverend Given finally loosened, squatted there close to his companions, still clinging to the long-barrelled rifle, and winked at Douglas.

'We are all born with the stain of original sin, Mister Ullman. Our everyday agonizing amounts to lifelong penance. Sometimes it ends very suddenly. Now you take them men down below where that little fire is. If the

Lord—His name be praised, amen—If the Lord decrees that you and me and this young man here, are to smite them cheek by jowl, then that is surely the will of God, and it is a good thing, because it means their everyday sufferings are over. We are the lambs of the Lord, Mister Ullman, are you plumb aware of that?'

Douglas sat like stone watching Dick Ullman wrestle with himself. It was clear Ullman was not a church-going man, and probably not a very religious man either. It was also clear that he had a fierce answer to all that preaching, right on the tip of his tongue. But he held it back.

Douglas finally turned and tried to make out the low fire down through the forest. He could not see it, but the incense-fragrance of dry, punky wood still came up to him, so the embers, at least, were still smouldering.

Ullman ignored the preacher and looked at Douglas as he said, 'One of us could skulk down there, more'n likely. They'll only have one man standin' guard.'

Douglas had his own ideas. 'We're not going to risk it, so settle back,' he told Ullman, and got a dark scowl back, which did not trouble him at all.

For a while they were quiet and still. A rodent-hunting owl, one of the prairie variety that lived in abandoned prairie-dog burrows under the ground, came skimming past. He was so intent on hunting he did not see the three men.

A wolf sang, just once, somewhere northward near

the black-rock cliffs. It was a booming, echoing sound, as unmistakably different from the cry of a coyote or the bark of a dog, as was the noise made by a horse and a mule.

The cold got no worse, down on the forest floor, but as the heavens began to lose their purple shadings, the stars shone dazzlingly brighter for a short while, meaning that it was much colder, if not down below, then certainly 'way up there.

Douglas sat wrapped in the old blanket-coat, his mind drifting back and forth, drifting back to the old days and old ways with Cade, then drifting easily forward to the times around North Fork, to the interludes when he had been with Angeline. He could close his eyes and see her smile and almost hear her laughter. It *was* her laughter! His eyes sprang wide, he saw the bushy-tailed big tree-squirrel sitting on the limb outside his hole half-way up the tree nearby, and listened to the squirrel's chattering sound that drowsiness had fooled Douglas into thinking was Angeline's laughter.

The squirrel was astonished at finding three men below in his private place, and he was also irate. He chattered for all he was worth, scolding them.

Douglas looked around, then unwound up to his feet. Dawn was very close. It had been just about an hour, as Reverend Given had said.

SIXTEEN

AN OUTLAW CAMP

Even Dick Ullman listened without comment when Douglas told his companions what came next. It was Weldon's life that he was putting on the line, not Ullman's nor Given's life.

'You know about where their camp is, so after I'm gone you can slip down closer and try to find a good place to get into position. Once you are close enough, be sure you're hidden. And don't shoot unless I do, or unless one of them offers to shoot me or the hostages. If the doctored whiskey works, there won't be any need for it. But keep ready. Find a good stand and keep your rifles aimed and cocked.' Douglas did not wait for questions. There were none that needed asking. Just before turning to depart he said, 'They're going to hear any sound from here on. Maybe you two had better shed your boots and go the rest of the way in your stocking feet.' He did not stress that, and a moment later he was gone through the trees with the watery paleness beginning to dilute all the curving rim of black velvet that followed round the horizon from west to east.

It was very easy for him to revert; the moment he had shed those clumping big boots back in town he felt lighter and had been able to move better. By now, coursing the dark forest soundlessly like a shadow, he could cover a lot of ground without rousing even the wakening animals.

It did not take long to get southward to the lip of a landswell where he had a good sighting of the swale where the outlaws had their camp. There was a glade nearby, a park around a seepage spring. The horses were over there; two cropping grass, the others drowsing. Douglas considered that, but stampeding the horses would only put the outlaws afoot at great jeopardy to the hostages. Evidently the Bentons were perfectly aware of this; it was very likely the reason they did not have anyone over in that little glade. But in any case, since the glade was less than fifty yards from the slightly depressed, circular place where the people were, a commotion over among the horses would have brought armed men on the run.

Where the dying fire showed twinkling red in its bed of ash, someone had made a stone fire-ring, which was customary. Saddles were upended, horns and swells to the ground, cantles upwards. Bridles had been draped from the upper ends and blankets, several turned to the fire, had been flung carelessly across the cantles. It resembled a cow-camp, in some ways. The people slept near the fire, rolled into blankets like cocoons, except for one man bundled in a sheep-pelt coat who was smoking and sipping coffee with his face to the fire and his back to one of the upended saddles. He had a Winchester leaning against one leg and his sixgun was well below the bottom of his coat. It was difficult to tell from where Douglas leaned in forest-gloom, looking, but this outlaw seemed no older than Douglas.

Whatever his age, that sentinel was the key to what Douglas had in mind, as his first effort. If he could be neutralized, the others would be at a disadvantage, even though they slept with their guns. The difficulty was that the forest ended some distance behind that man, and by simply palming his Colt and turning his head anyone trying to reach him across the clearing would furnish him with a perfect target.

Douglas abandoned the idea. He did not want to create any kind of crisis if that could be avoided. Next, he studied the blanketrolls trying to discern Angeline, but the light was still too poor. There were six people lying round the stone-ring. Counting the sentinel there were seven people in the outlaw-camp. As the light improved he could make out two that definitely were men, but while he was trying to define the others, one of the blanketrolls moved, twisted round and a man sat up, yawned, spat into the ash and looked around for his hat. From the sentinel came a quiet greeting.

'Quiet as the grave.'

The awakened man did not seem to be in the best of moods, as few men were when they were first roused from sleep. 'That's a hell of a way to put it,' he growled, and flung his blanket aside as he ran a hand over a leathery, stubbled face. 'Set the coffee to boiling and I'll take m'carbine and hike down a ways to see if anyone's on the road.'

'Ain't no one down there,' said the sentinel, getting stiffly to his feet, muscles stiff from cold. 'I went and looked a few minutes ago. Too dark anyway.' He took the Winchester with him as he crossed to the fire to poke it to life. 'If they don't show up by ten o'clock, we'd better shift this camp across the road to the east side. Better horse-feed over there.'

The newly awakened man got to his feet saying, 'Horse-feed, hell.' He picked up a saddle-gun and went pacing across the little depression and up its far side, where he stood a moment, then he went farther out.

The camp came to life slowly. Douglas cast a look at the sky, which was rapidly fading from its night-time gloom. The sun was still somewhere below the eastern horizon, but pastel false-dawn was over the land making it steely blue.

Douglas did not wait any longer. He turned and went back the way he had come without leaving a track of any kind upon the spongy layer of needles. When he was able to spot Ullman and Given farther off and slightly apart from one another, he considered their stand. It was adequate; both men were almost entirely hidden. Douglas did not acknowledge them, he veered to the west and strode in that direction for a while, then reversed himself and started back.

He made noise, but not a lot of it, and once, when a squirrel scolded, he laughed and called it a name as he passed beneath its perch.

Closer, he stopped to take a sip from one of the bottles. Whiskey was bad enough any time, but on an empty stomach first thing in the morning, it was worse. He did not swallow much, just enough to smell of it, then he started onward again, Cade's long-barrelled rifle hooked carelessly in the bend of one arm while he clumsily worked at re-corking the bottle. This was how he wanted them to see him first, and it worked.

Drawn by the noise, two men appeared, about twenty feet apart, one with a Colt, one with a carbine. Douglas saw them before he let them know it. They were watching his swinging approach like carved statues, evidently trying to fathom who he was and where he had come from.

It was easy, when he finally raised his head from the work with the bottle, to pretend astonishment. He stopped, stared, then pushed the bottle into his coat and made a slower, more concerned examination of the strangers. One was beginning to grey at the temples, the other man was younger. He had been the sentinel Douglas had been watching earlier.

The greying man had sharp, narrow features and deepset grey eyes. He kept his sixgun aimed at Douglas's middle as he said, 'Who in hell are you?'

Douglas told the truth. 'Name's Douglas Cade

Weldon.' He jerked his head backwards. 'Got a place up on Cade's mountain.' He paused as though awaiting a reciprocal introduction, and when it failed to materialize he said, 'You boys riding through?'

The younger outlaw let his Winchester barrel droop a little, which was encouraging, but the greying man continued to study Douglas. But the trapper-coat, the worn moccasins, the general appearance and that long-barrelled old rifle could not be faulted. They were not actually a disguise anyway, they had been worn or carried only about a month earlier in all sincerity. The greying man did not lower his pistol but when next he spoke his voice was a shade different, less sharp and wary.

'How come you to pass along this way, and where was you going?'

Douglas leaned on Cade's rifle. 'You ask a lot of questions, mister. I came down this way because it's handy to the road. I'll wait down there until a stage comes along, then I won't have to walk all the way to North Fork. And that's where I'm going, to North Fork, the town south of here a ways.' Douglas smiled a little. 'Springtime's here, mister. Maybe a man can get some orders for hunting meat. There'll be no trapping again until winter comes back.'

A third man came walking back. He studied Douglas as he approached the greying outlaw. This newcomer was in age somewhere between the youth with the carbine and the greying man. He looked mean and vicious.

'Coffee's ready,' he growled, then jutted his jaw at Douglas. 'What you got here, new-generation Mountain Man? He's a trapper, I can tell from here. You can smell 'em this far.'

The greying man finally loosened his stance and let the Colt-barrel sag, but he did not put the weapon up. He used it to gesture with. 'Walk on past,' he told Douglas, sounding disgruntled now, not menacing. 'That bottle— hand it over.'

Douglas moved ahead, then scowled at the outlaw's demand. 'Don't mind sharing a drink with you,' he told the greying man, 'but be damned if I'll give you the bottle.'

The vicious-faced outlaw stepped out and blocked Douglas's way. With one hand on his holstered gun and the other hand extended, he said, 'The bottle.' Douglas halted ten feet away. He looked back. The other two were closing in on him. He pulled forth a bottle and handed it over. 'That's one hell of a way to treat folks you meet on the trail,' he snapped, showing honest dislike for the vicious-looking man.

The greying outlaw moved on past as he said, 'We're going to trade with you, trapper. You can have some of our coffee and fried venison for breakfast.'

Douglas followed the greying man. The other two stayed behind. In this manner Douglas arrived in the outlaw-camp. He saw Gabriel Longstreet and Alex Farraday working on their knees at the fire. Angeline was nowhere in sight, and neither was one of the other out-laws. Not at first, anyway, not until Douglas got down the slight incline, then he saw her over where a little creek meandered. He had missed seeing that creek in the darkness. She arose and turned, her face shiny with creek-water. Douglas made a point of looking away, then he looked back, and she had recovered from the surprise and was drying her face and hands. He had always thought her father and Longstreet would be able to keep impassive faces when he appeared in the outlaw-camp, but he had entertained doubts that she'd be able to, and this was very important. She started slowly over to the fire, with its rising smoke and good heat, without casting another look at Douglas. He thought she carried it off very well.

Farraday and Longstreet were the cooks. One of them filled a dented tin cup with coffee and handed it upwards. Douglas accepted it with thanks, and looked steadily into the eyes of the donor. That lasted a moment, was all.

Food smelled good. So did smoke from a cooking-fire. In the east there was a quick, hard blaze of orange. The sun popped up like the seed being squirted from a grape. The outlaws moved almost indifferently among their hostages. They seemed to scorn both Longstreet and Farraday, which was understandable. Neither of those townsmen were gun-handy. It was doubtful that either of them had carried a gun in years, if ever.

They did not seem to feel any different towards Angeline. The greying one looked at her now and then, and the youngest outlaw also showed some masculine interest, but the other two hardly acknowledged her presence. They were between the ages of the greying and the youngest outlaw. One was the vicious-looking outlaw, the other one had a flushed, puffy face and quick, darting pale eyes.

Douglas guessed the youngest man and the greying outlaw were the Bentons. The younger one looked a lot like the Benton who had been shot to death not far from here. The dead man had been a little younger, perhaps, otherwise the likeness was remarkable.

Douglas did not try to guess which of those four men was the deadliest. Surely, the young outlaw would be fast. The greying one, that younger man's brother, would be the quickest to suspect anything. The other two, probably along for pay, would be like striking rattlesnakes. It would be a toss-up which of them would react first and fastest, if trouble came.

Little was said until the men had eaten. The vicious-faced outlaw kept his appropriated whiskey bottle at his side where they squatted. He and the other one, who was not a Benton, sat together, eating in dour silence.

From time to time the outlaws looked covertly at Douglas, who squatted close by eating the tough doe-meat, alert to everything, and everyone, around him.

It was the most bizarre breakfast Douglas or any of

the hostages had ever eaten, and none of them acted very hungry.

The attitude of the outlaws had to be as much related to their impatience, as at the arrival in their camp of the mountaineer. Either way, whether three men rode out singly from North Fork, or not, before this day ended the Bentons were going to commit murder.

S E V E N T E E N

THREE CAPTIVES WITHOUT A SHOT

The greying man left without a word, after he had eaten. He took along his saddle-gun and stalked southward beyond the rise at the far, lower end of the little depression where the camp was. He did not have to say where he was going.

Douglas was acutely aware of this man's departure. He would have much preferred having them all in front of him. The vicious-faced man snarled at Farraday and Longstreet to scrub the pans and tin plates at the little creek, then he settled an unfriendly but masked gaze upon Douglas. 'Any Injuns back in these mountains?' he asked, and lay a hand upon the unopened whiskey bottle.

Douglas forced himself not to look down at the bottle when he answered. He had been forcing himself not to look at Angeline since that first glimpse, but now he knew she was watching him.

'Maybe a few, but just hunters this time of year. In wintertime they sometimes trap lower down. I haven't seen many in the highlands in ten years.'

The outlaw's brow creased. 'Ten years? How long you been up in here?'

Douglas answered truthfully. 'Nearly all my life. I have a cabin northwest of here about thirty miles.'

'You *walked* thirty miles through these gawddamned mountains?' asked the outlaw, looking incredulous.

Douglas smiled. 'I've walked a lot more miles than that. There are plenty of places back in there where a man can camp overnight and be as comfortable as he'd be in a hotel in town.'

The vicious-faced man pondered on that, still holding the laudanum-laced whiskey by the neck of the bottle. 'Suppose some fellers wanted to lose themselves back up there . . . ?'

Douglas could answer that easily. 'No problem at all. The thing would be not to really get lost. There are something like two hundred miles of rough country between the North Fork prairie and the range-country on the far side. I've heard tales of men wandering round and round up in there—and leaving their bones under some tree.'

The other outlaw, the puffy-faced man, said, 'But a posse could comb them hills, couldn't it?'

Douglas had no trouble guessing the way these men's minds were running. 'Not unless the posse had a feller outriding for it who knew the uplands. Two hundred miles is a couple of weeks' riding, in that kind of country, mister, even on strong horses. And a posse as big as an army could ride within a hundred yards of a hidden camp and never see it—providing the fellers in the camp knew where to set up, and how to keep out of sight.' Douglas reached, filled his tin cup with coffee again, and made a face when he tasted the black liquid. It was as bitter as green acorns.

The vicious-faced man suddenly arose and went stalking down in the direction the greying man had disappeared. His whiskey bottle was left unattended. The puffy-faced man eyed the bottle and swallowed a couple of times, then he darted a snake-quick look over where the youngest outlaw was shaping up a smoke, his hat tilted back, sitting cross-legged directly opposite Angeline. As the man lit up, he lay a meaningful look on the girl and smiled softly as he blew smoke. Angeline purposefully looked away, looked at Douglas. He returned the gaze with stony impassivity.

The puffy-faced man finally weakened and reached for the bottle. The younger Benton said, 'You take it easy with that stuff. Scot will slit your ear and pull your arm through it if you get tanked again.'

Douglas felt his stomach draw up tight as the puffy-faced outlaw worried loose the cap. If that man took a big drink, and passed out within a few minutes, which would certainly happen, before his friends had also taken a big drink, it wouldn't take the others more than a moment to guess that was not ordinary whiskey in the bottle.

He said, 'Pass it around,' to the puffy-faced man. 'Give the other fellers a chance at it.'

He might as well have saved his breath. He was speaking to a chronic drinker. Angeline, looking closely at Douglas, seemed to wonder about something; she had that kind of a look on her face. He ignored her and watched in fascination as the outlaw moistened his lips with a pink tongue, then raised the bottle. The younger Benton also watched. After the drinker's Adams-apple had bobbed twice, young Benton's arm shot out like a striking snake, caught hold of the bottle and spilled some of its contents as he wrenched it away.

The puffy-faced man's darting eyes turned murderous. He said, 'Hand it back, Al.'

Young Benton smiled, the bottle in his left fist, his right hand resting lightly upon a leg within inches of his holstered Colt. 'Make me,' he taunted. 'You drunken bastard, Cramer.'

Douglas held his breath. For five seconds he was sure the man called Cramer was going to draw and fire. Apparently Cramer knew something about young Benton's handiness with a gun that deterred him. Cramer let his hand drop and said, 'All right. Take a drink, then I'll have another one. Just one.'

Young Benton continued to taunt the older man with

his cruel grin. He suddenly shoved the bottle towards Douglas. 'Have a drink, trapper.' Benton was doing this deliberately; he wanted to prolong Cramer's suffering. Douglas accepted the bottle, set it to his mouth and worked his throat as though swallowing then he handed the bottle, not to Benton, but across to Cramer.

Benton lunged to interfere and Douglas eluded him without effort. Cramer took the bottle and twisted sideways as he raised it. Young Benton got red in the face. He glared at Douglas. But when he moved, it was towards the drinking man, and again he tore loose the bottle. That time, though, Cramer yielded it without a struggle. He smiled at Benton, showing bad teeth.

The other two were returning. They walked heads-down and muttering back and forth. When the greying man came up, and hunkered, he shot a venomous look at Alex Farraday, who was near Douglas. If ever a man showed death in his expression, it was the greying man.

'No one's on the road,' he exclaimed, and twisted to include Gabe Longstreet in his lethal stare. 'Your friends down there are going to get you killed, boys.'

Longstreet spoke up. 'We told you—so did other folks back in town—the cowboys who rode out when your brother got killed left the country two weeks ago. They aren't *down* there. How can you expect anyone to take their place?'

'Well, someone better take their place,' snarled the greying man, and looked around when his brother

nudged him and offered the bottle. He took it. Douglas had not been watching so he did not know whether the youngest Benton had drunk or not. But the elder Benton drank. He pulled down three big swallows, then carelessly handed the bottle to the vicious-faced man as he turned and resumed his tirade against Longstreet.

'You go first—feet down, mister. I don't give a gawddamn whether the fellers who was in on my brother's killin' left North Fork or not. It's the *town* that needs a lesson, and so help me Chriz' it's going to get one.'

Benton breathed hard. To Douglas it was abundantly clear that this older man was the deadliest one. Benton suddenly said, 'Trapper, you said you knew these mountains good enough to hide folks without 'em ever being found. Well; your lousy life depends on whether you was lyin' or tellin' the truth. We're going to set around here another hour, then we're going to let you take us to a good place with feed and water, where we can't be found not if the whole damned U.S. Army comes searching. Can you do that?'

Douglas nodded without speaking. He and the elder Benton looked long at one another. Then Benton's ferocity left and he smiled. 'We ain't riders just passing through, are we? You figured out who we are by now, haven't you?'

Douglas answered that carefully. 'You're in some kind of trouble.'

The greying man laughed. 'Naw hell, *we're* not.

These here people we took as hostages from North Fork, *they're* the ones in trouble. If some riders don't come up that road soon now, these folks are going to get shot in the head and sent back home tied belly-down on their saddles. Now, trapper, wouldn't you say *they* are the ones in trouble?'

Douglas drew out the other whiskey bottle, worried the cap off and raised the thing to take a swallow. Benton laughed again. He jeered. 'Hey boys, look at the mountaineer; his gawddamned guts just come all un-strung inside him.'

Douglas lowered the bottle, felt Angeline's eyes on him, and put the bottle in the dirt in front of where he was hunkering. 'You figuring to kill the girl too?' he asked.

Benton nodded, eyes drawing out narrow. 'Trapper, don't get ideas. There's four of us. But if there was only one, someone like you wouldn't be in the same league.'

Douglas saw the puffy-faced man start to roll a smoke and spill half the tobacco. He did not want the others to notice that. 'Look,' he said to the elder Benton, 'I don't give a damn what trouble you fellers are in—can't no one find you if I take it into my head to make sure they don't . . . Mister, you kill that girl and I won't lead you one damned step away from this camp.'

Both Bentons looked surprised. The trapper they had already pegged as a dissolute coward, was turning out not to be so cowardly after all. The vicious-faced outlaw sneered. 'You want to die with her?'

Douglas flicked his glance to this man. 'You want to end up riding your horses to death going in circles back in those mountains?'

The younger Benton broke the sudden cold silence by saying, 'Don't worry about *her,* trapper. No one's going to kill her.' He caught the quick, savage look his brother threw his way, and modified that statement. 'Not yet. Not for a long while yet.'

The puffy-faced man raised his hump-backed cigarette to lick the edge of the paper before closing it, and broke the thing letting paper and tobacco spill down his front. They all saw that, even Farraday and Longstreet and Angeline. Young Benton swore. 'Damned tramp; he took three, four swallows before I could get the bottle away from him. Now look. What the hell good is he? I told you he was worthless.'

The elder Benton's stare was deadly. Douglas felt his muscles tightening. This was like being in a den of rabid wolves; worse, rabid wolves were blind, these men were able to see, to direct their fury, along with being just as murderous.

The vicious-faced man leaned and looked closely. 'Cramer,' he said, 'what's the matter with you?' To the Bentons he shook his head. 'Hell; Cramer don't get sloppy drunk on no four or five swallows of whiskey.'

'Don't he?' snarled the elder Benton. 'What do *you* call that?'

Douglas raised his head. 'Listen. Shut up a minute.' He hadn't heard anything but it worked, the others all stopped moving and speaking. Young Benton arose with a Winchester in one fist and without a word went quickly southward past the fire-ring and towards the far lift of the campsite. Beyond, where trees formed a screening barrier, he passed from sight with a long, swinging stride.

Douglas had sweat running under his shirt and it was not that warm. He offered the bottle of whiskey from in front of him to the elder Benton. He wanted Benton to reach for it with his right hand. But Benton shook his head. The vicious-faced man thrust out a hand though, and as Douglas handed over the bottle with his left hand, his right hand dipped and rose.

Benton saw what was happening too late. He still tried, though, but his hand missed the saw-handle grip and when he pulled it back Douglas's weapon made its metal-on-metal, cocking sound.

The vicious-faced outlaw was caught with the whiskey bottle in his gunhand. He almost dropped it, but the Colt barrel across from him, covering Benton, looked too close, far too deadly. He let his arm down slowly and set the bottle at his feet.

Cramer fell forward in a broken-over slump.

Alex Farraday reached far over and disarmed the elder Benton. Longstreet moved gingerly behind the other man and lifted away his gun too. No one said a word. Benton was staring at Douglas Weldon as though he could not believe this was happening. Then he raised a hand and rubbed his eyes, and blew out a big, unsteady breath. 'What the hell was in that whiskey?' he asked thickly.

The vicious-faced man turned to stare. Benton could not keep his eyes open. With dawning understanding the vicious-faced outlaw turned back to slowly stare at Douglas, then out behind him, up through the trees where two flitting silhouettes were approaching from tree to tree. The outlaw said, 'Gawd—damn!' and drifted his stunned gaze back to Douglas.

Benton fell sideways, striking the other outlaw, who moved away and let Benton go all the way to the ground.

E I G H T E E N

AN ENDING

Douglas was on his feet in one jump. He hardly waited for Given and Ullman to hasten forward where even the toughest of the drugged outlaws, the vicious-faced man, was beginning to find it hard to sit up and keep his eyes open.

Farraday and Longstreet were gathering up weapons when Ullman and the preacher came down out of the trees and into the outlaw-camp. Farraday said, 'Dick, get ropes from the saddles and let's tie them.'

Douglas had no illusions about how long the younger Benton would remain down there watching the road. It was possible to see all the way to town on a clear day, like this, and if no rider was coming, then obviously, there was not going to be a rider. Young Benton would come back soon, and the moment he appeared upon the lip of land overlooking the camp, he would start shooting.

Angeline intercepted him. 'Wait! Don't go into the trees alone!'

He put out an arm to gently push her aside. The others were fully occupied with the drugged outlaws. There was no time to spare. 'Stay here,' he told her. 'Stay down here with the others.' On the spur of the moment he ducked down and met her lips coming up in a swift peck of a kiss. At that precise moment Alexander Farraday glanced round for his daughter. Then Douglas hurried past, up the far slope and without a pause passed through the first fringe of trees.

It was as still, as hushed and silent in the forest as it usually was. Not even a bird scolded from overhead where sunlight was trying to burn though to the forest's matting.

Douglas made a quick examination for boot-marks, saw several, all going due south in the same direction, and glided off to one side as he foraged ahead. The younger Benton, like the others, had probably one fixed vantage point down through here where they could see the roadway best. Probably too, having gone down there together at one time or another, they would all return to that same place.

At least the sign read that way. Douglas kept to the right of it, to the west, and he did not hasten once he was protected by the sheltering trees. He had already made his judgment of the younger Benton; the only way Douglas could make a capture would be if he could come in, unexpectedly, behind Benton. And even then he was not sure the outlaw would not try to make a fight of it. Men with little to lose once in captivity, were conditioned to take long chances to avoid being captured.

The sunlight reached downward where the forest began to thin out, lower down towards the prairie. Douglas went over to read the sign again, then continued on where the trees were farther apart.

He saw Benton.

The outlaw was pacing to the left, which was eastward, and coming up the distant roadway was a solitary rider. Douglas halted a moment to make a study of that horseman. It might be someone from town, and it might be just some unsuspecting traveller, but whoever he was, without a doubt he was shortly to get the surprise of his life, unless Douglas could get close enough behind Benton first.

The outlaw was moving easily. He was a lithe, supple man. He never once glanced back; his full attention was upon that oncoming horseman.

Douglas took every advantage in order to close the distance. He cursed the sixgun on his thigh, wishing he'd brought Old Cade's dragoon pistol with the twelve-inch barrel. With that weapon he would never have had to get any closer than he was now, and if Benton made a fight of it, Benton's six-inch barrel would have been no match. But wishing was not going to change anything.

Benton left the trees for a dozen or so yards and hiked boldly towards the roadway in plain sight. It was improbable that the horseman could see him, though, because, aside from the sun's blinding brilliance, Benton had the forest at his back.

Douglas had to dog-trot to try and close the distance separating them. The rider was in no hurry. His horse was slogging along, head down and reins swinging. If he was some volunteer martyr from town, then it was quite understandable that he was in no hurry.

Young Benton got to within a hundred yards of the road, stopped behind a tree, then, when Douglas was stepping gingerly forward, the outlaw went quickly another few yards closer to the roadway and sank from sight, all but the crown of his hat, amid some big boulders. Douglas saw the hat move as the oncoming rider suddenly reined up, out there, and sat staring. Evidently the stranger had seen Benton drop down in those rocks.

Douglas could hear his heart pounding as he moved stealthily closer and got within thirty yards of the rocks, seeking an opening to one side or the other that would allow him a good sighting.

The place where Benton had entered the natural fortification was northward. By the time Douglas could glide up there and look down in, could see the crouched and waiting outlaw, the horseman was urging his mount forward again. Without a doubt, he was someone from town; no stranger in his right mind, after he had seen a skulking man hide in some rocks ahead of him on a road, would continue in the same direction.

Douglas tested the ground. There was less matting out here where the trees were farther apart, and more shale-stone that slithered underfoot. In boots Douglas would never have accomplished it, but he got up to within twenty yards and had a good view of the outlaw, without making a sound. He called softly as he reached for his Colt.

'Benton! Freeze where you are!'

Perhaps, if Douglas had tried a ruse, it would have worked. The outlaw had no reason to expect to see anyone behind him but his own brother, or his outlaw-companions. The idea of a ruse never crossed Douglas's mind. When he called, he was prepared for what ensued.

Young Benton's head whipped around. He saw Douglas at once even though there was a tree and its thin shadow to one side of Douglas. Benton went for his gun. He was fast, very fast in fact. He had the weapon clear of leather when Douglas fired.

The bullet hit Benton hard, broke him backwards

against a solid granite escarpment, and although he bounced off and came up erect, as though he were uninjured, the gun slid to the shale at his feet, and one moment later Benton fell across it.

Out on the stageroad that horseman was down on the off-side of his mount with a glistening Winchester resting across the saddle-seat. But he had no target. Neither Benton, who was face down in rock dust, nor Douglas Weldon, the man who had shot Benton, was in the newcomer's view.

For as long as the echoes chased one another outwards across the open country neither Douglas nor the stranger moved, but that did not last long. The gunshot had startled a feeding deer; it went bouncing in stiff-legged flight from the trees southward into plain sight on the prairie. Otherwise, as Douglas started towards the rocks where Benton lay, there was no movement.

Benton was not dead but the bullet had pierced his upper chest and it was Douglas's guess that he would be bleeding internally. Barring pneumonia or other complications, most men survived lung shots of this kind. Douglas knew from experience as a trapper and hunter that as long as the slug made a clean entrance and exit, death did not have to follow.

He raised up with Benton's weapons and saw that the rider was angling off the road towards him. Without any idea who the rider was, Douglas welcomed his arrival, but when the man saw Douglas and called his name, even though he was still a little far off to recognize, Douglas knew him.

Mike Clancy.

They met just beyond the rocks and Douglas explained about young Benton, and as Clancy got down to stroll over and peer downward, Douglas also explained what else had occurred. Clancy leaned on the warm stone, tipped down his hatbrim against sunglare and acted very relieved but not terribly surprised.

'We figured something like this was afoot when you'n Dick and Reverend Given wasn't in town this morning. The three best shots. Johnathon was fit to be tied.' Clancy smiled. 'I told him doing *anything* was better than doing nothing, but I don't think he agreed with me. So, I rode out.'

'They would have shot you,' Douglas said, and watched the older man's affable expression turn sardonic.

'Maybe. But I got a derringer hid in each boot and a knife strapped round me under my shirt. That's beside the regular sixgun and carbine. The more I figured on it this morning the more it seemed like you three fellers needed one more hand to even things up.' Clancy turned and gazed down again. 'And it turns out you didn't. Well; how about this one?'

'High on the right side through the lights,' explained Douglas. 'Can't take him back on a horse.'

Clancy agreed. 'Sure can't. Maybe I'd ought to go on

back and fetch a wagon out here. Any other hurt ones?'

Douglas grinned. 'Unconscious but not hurt. They'd all be easier to handle if we had a wagon.'

Clancy walked over and caught the reins of his horse. 'Go tell Dick and the preacher to get a little rest. It'll take a while.' Clancy smiled thoughtfully from the saddle. 'You know, Johnathon and I talked this morning; seems that although you kept refusin' to act as town marshal, you been doing the work all the same.' Clancy turned and loped southward on an angle that would eventually put him back on the road.

Douglas returned to young Benton, who was still unconscious and who seemed likely to remain that way for some time. Haemorrhaging or not, there was nothing Douglas could do, and in fact probably the best thing was to leave him where he was, unmoving and shaded, until the wagon came out from town.

Douglas started back towards the camp, but on a different course; he was sure everything was under control back there, but it never hurt to be cautious.

The day was well enough advanced by now for heat, even in the forest, to be noticeable. It was still springtime, otherwise it would have been much hotter. He passed in and out of shadows and sunspots, crossed a grassy place, came to the east-west rib of land that formed the southernmost lip of that depression up where the outlaw-camp was, and angled along it heading west until he could distinctly scent a dying fire mixed with a boiling-coffee fragrance. From where he was then, trees obscured the view, but he twisted back and forth through them and finally saw the camp.

Even without any bindings Scot Benton, Cramer, and Cramer's partner would have been helpless. They were lying stretched out in tree-shade like corpses placed in a row.

Farraday, Longstreet, the preacher and Dick Ullman were talking near the fire, and where Angeline was standing, slightly apart looking steadily southward into the forest where Douglas had disappeared, sunshine made her hair glow blue-black.

Douglas stepped into her view and without a sound she ran out to him. Her father and the others turned, watched, and said nothing. They did not have to ask, anyway, Douglas was carrying young Benton's guns.

Angeline's face was flushed from the heat, and from running. She clutched his arm and said, 'I never prayed so hard in my life. There was just one shot. I wanted to run out there but the others wouldn't let me. They were so certain about everything.'

Douglas slid an arm round her supple waist. 'Mike Clancy came along. He went back for a wagon. Young Benton's hit through the lights, but he'll probably make it.' He squeezed, hard, then loosened his grip as he saw the four men watching. Finally, he released her alto-gether, except for a hand. They walked the balance of the way holding hands. Where he stopped, within a yard or two of the older men, he explained again about that solitary gunshot, and about Clancy's arrival and departure. Then he said, 'That ends it, I reckon.'

The older men agreed that it seemed to be ended. Ullman pointed to a pair of whiskey bottles sitting side-by-side in the sunlight over near the stone-ring. 'Which is which?' he asked. 'These fellers and I could stand a jolt or two.'

Douglas winked at Angeline and turned to walk over and look at the doped prisoners. 'Darned if I remember, Mister Ullman.'

Ullman's neck swelled and his face reddened. Gabe Longstreet tapped him on the shoulder. 'Wouldn't do you one damned bit of harm to learn to laugh at jokes on yourself, Dick.'

Ullman glared. 'What is so funny about me with a parched throat, and that damned young whippersnapper teasing his elders? I'll tell you for a fact, old Campbell's right; this upcoming generation don't have the respect; you got to have respect and decent manners if this world's to progress. By gawd I'm afraid what the world's going to be like in another forty, fifty years, and that is a plumb fact!'

NINETEEN

CADE'S TRAIL WITHOUT END

Douglas could not avoid thinking how he would have been received back in town if things up in the foothills had happened differently.

Good intentions were never enough. He learned that as he entered town with the others, riding on each side of Clancy's wagon, leading spare horses. The best intentions in the world could still have got Angeline and her father, as well as Gabe Longstreet, killed, and if that had happened . . .

Douglas acknowledged the cheers and waves. People lined the dusty roadway. It had been a very long night for everyone, even for the folks back in town who hadn't actually had a stake in the trouble.

He was softly smiling when Angeline leaned and said, 'You are their hero as well as my hero,' and laughed when he frowned at her.

Alex Farraday and Gabe Longstreet stood out front when Ullman and the others including Mike Clancy, called for help to carry the drugged outlaws inside to a cell. Farraday and Longstreet siphoned off most of the curious people who thronged in from all sides for the details, and that gave Douglas and Angeline a chance to go inside and speak with Johnathon Barlow, who watched impassively as the elder Benton was carried in, along with his companions, and placed on the floor in the next-door cell. When the younger Benton was brought in on a stretcher made of a blanket, and deposited on the bunk next door, Marshal Barlow craned his neck until Douglas and Angeline arrived, then he looked sceptically upwards.

'Who else got shot?' he asked Douglas.

Angeline answered. 'No one. Douglas and Dick Ullman put laudanum in a bottle of whiskey.'

Barlow looked at Douglas. 'Laudanum? That stuff the dentist gives you before he pulls a fang?'

Douglas pulled up the little bench for Angeline before answering. 'The same stuff. The idea came to me yesterday. Old Cade kept a bottle handy at the cabin. Good for a toothache and such like, he claimed. He showed me how much to use—otherwise he said sometimes folks don't come out of it; they slip right on over into the Sand Hills without ever awakening.' Douglas leaned on the steel bars and gazed through into the adjoining cell. 'The young one's shot through the lung. Dick Ullman said he'll do what he can.'

Barlow looked over there too, at the inert, pale man on the bunk. 'Bullet stop or go on through?'

'It went through.'

Barlow looked back as though dismissing young Benton from his mind. 'He'll likely make it, although that may not be a real gift. He and his brother are wanted

in Arizona and Colorado and Texas. Gabe and Alex all right?'

Douglas nodded.

Barlow glanced over at Angeline a moment, then said, 'By golly, Angie, you look *better.*'

She did not answer, she only smiled.

Several men drifted in to ogle the prisoners. More would probably have come but Ullman appeared in the cell-room doorway growling in his most disagreeable voice for everyone to clear out. They did, and not a one of them offered an argument. Ullman was rumpled and unshaven and more bear-like than ever. When the crowd melted he looked in at Johnathon, at Angeline and Douglas, and winked. Then he moved ahead to the cell next-door and knelt at the bunk. His back was so broad it was impossible to see what he was doing, but whatever it was had to do with the younger Benton, nor would it have made much difference if Dick had been a fully qualified physician, for that kind of wound rest, quiet, and the natural healing processes were the only things that would determine whether young Benton lived or died.

Barlow said, 'I would have stopped you if I could have,' to young Weldon, then wagged his head. 'And I'd have been wrong—but no one would have ever known it, would they?'

Douglas looked at Angeline. He was tired, not as much from the long, arduous night, as from the worry that had been eating on him since he had first left town with Given and Ullman the previous night.

He did not answer Barlow. The question, like the idea it propounded, had no answer. He held out a hand and drew Angeline to her feet. 'We'll look in on you later,' he told Marshal Barlow, and left, still holding Angeline by the hand.

Outside, people were talking in little groups, not only in front of the jailhouse, but also on both sides of the roadway, north and south. Some would have attempted to halt Douglas and Alex Farraday's daughter, but Douglas nodded without smiling and kept right on walking. He got her all the way up to Elm Street, and turned right, before they ran out of people. He was still clutching her hand, too.

Elm Street looked so orderly and proper and civilized. He admired the houses, the wide front porches, the glass windows, and when he released her hand, finally, not far from the Farraday residence, he said, 'I'll tell you something: I feel more foreign right now, today, than I felt that first day when Dick Ullman almost ran me off.'

She was surprised and stopped at the stone walkway leading to the front porch to look up at him. 'Why?'

He wasn't sure. 'Maybe, because—look at me; I'm dressed exactly as I was that first day—and now they can't pat me hard enough on the back. And all I did, Angeline, was do what Cade taught me: Out-figure the varmint you're trying to trap.'

She reached and put a cool palm against his cheek. Then she said, 'Come in. I'll make some coffee . . . and lace it for you the way I sometimes do for my father, and we'll sit for a spell.'

He declined. 'Maybe tomorrow. Right now I'd like to float in the river with a bar of soap, then go lie under a shade-tree and sleep for ten hours.' He smiled. 'Something happened up there. I could have taken young Benton without shooting, I think . . . I didn't think of it.'

'But that's understandable, Douglas.'

'Not the way you mean,' he stated. 'I didn't think of it, Angie, because I didn't *want* to take him that way. Remember how he looked at you—the things he said when his brother was talking about killing the hostages?'

She nodded, her eyes widening in gradual understanding.

'Well; that's why I didn't want to take him alive. I had in mind killing him when I left camp and went looking for him.' Douglas met her black, steady gaze for a moment, then spoke again. 'A man learns things, Angie. Old Cade used to say life was a trail without end. He was sure right. I've never wanted to kill a man before this morning. It was a lesson. I'm glad he didn't die . . . Well; reckon I'd better be hiking along.' He hesitated. 'Maybe, if men didn't wear guns, a lot of things would come and go, and turn out not to amount to much, that otherwise get men buried.'

As he turned she said, 'Douglas,' and raised both arms to his shoulders, right out there in plain sight, and pulled him to her as she stood very erect to reach his lips. After the kiss, she dropped down and said, 'Come back,' and with her black eyes softly liquid, she turned and ran to the porch and entered the house.

He went trudging back towards the centre of town, and turned off towards the hotel hardly seeing the people who looked frankly and amiably at him. Upstairs, he was able to look down into the roadway and see those same people, see the busy jailhouse, see Gabe Longstreet striding homeward with his wife, see Mike Clancy and Dick Ullman leading a file of thirsty men up in the direction of the Montana House, where Ullman would probably hold forth for at least an hour, downing drinks.

And for the first time Douglas smiled at the town; for the first time he felt that he belonged.

He and Angie went buggy-riding the following afternoon. That night they went down to visit the prisoners. The younger Benton had been moved out back to a storeroom because Dick had said he needed more privacy and quiet. He looked flushed, and there was a hawk-faced greying woman standing with crossed arms when Douglas and Angeline entered the little room. She nodded, but in an unrelenting manner, and said, 'No conversation; he's not allowed to talk. Those are Mister Ullman's orders.'

Benton and Douglas Weldon exchanged a look. Douglas smiled, and the wounded man smiled back. That was the extent of it.

After they were outside, with the nurse being certain the door was closed, Angeline said, 'He looks—fair—doesn't he?'

Douglas nodded, and they went back through to the cell where the other three outlaws were locked in. Here, their welcome was cold and bitter. Scot Benton looked venomously out through the bars. Cramer and the vicious-faced man showed antagonism, but it was mixed with a sullenness that kept them from meeting Douglas's gaze. Only Benton spoke. He walked ahead to the front of the cell and said, 'Mister, if I ever get out, I'll be back for you.'

Douglas, mindful of Angeline beside him, simply nodded. Then he moved on as far as the cell where Marshal Barlow was sitting up. Barlow had heard that remark by Benton, and his expression was dour. Speaking loud enough for Benton to hear, Barlow said, 'Just talk, Douglas. Just talk. I've had a hundred of them make that same threat, and so far not a one ever came back. But North Fork can afford to wait, if this one wants to make it good. Only—he's the least likely one to be able to do it. They want him for more crimes than you can shake a stick at.' Barlow changed the subject. 'I'll be able to stand up and move around a little in another week.' He studied Douglas for a moment. 'Are you figuring on staying around?'

Douglas smiled because Angeline's hand surreptitiously found his hand, behind them, and clung tightly. 'I reckon so, Marshal.'

Barlow was not surprised at all. 'I had it in mind that you would,' he said, dryly.

They left without asking what the lawman had meant by that. It did not really matter anyway. Not right then, anyway.

Dusk came a little later this particular evening, as Douglas walked Angeline homeward, but they did not stop at her house, they strolled on, with the pleasant night closing down behind them a little at a time, and went all the way down to the river.

The moon had been full, and had gone dark, and was now building again towards fullness. It was a high crescent, and Douglas smiled as he recalled something. 'No rain for a while. If the lower horn of the moon is tilted enough so's a powder-horn will hang from it, it will rain. That moon up there, well, it's almost straight up and down, so the powder-horn would fall off. That means it won't rain.'

She looked up. 'Old Cade . . . ?'

He looked down into her lifted face. 'Old Cade. You'll get tired of listening to that kind of talk.'

She moved her head a little, settling a dark look on him. 'Not from you, I won't. Not ever.' She waited.

Someone came walking down the slope at their back

and Douglas sighed with mild exasperation. This was no time for an interruption. It was a lanky young boy with a coal-oil lantern, unlit, and a wicked, pronged trident. He was going frogging. There was an old belief that the best frogging was done in the first quarter of a new moon. The boy looked at them with frank and lively curiosity, then nodded and hiked right on past, heading up the riverbank north of town.

Angeline laughed softly at Douglas's expression. She tugged at his fingers heading back up the bank towards Elm Street. 'It's always too crowded,' she murmured. 'Up there in the outlaw-camp or down here in town. Too many people. Too many interruptions.'

In the northeasterly distance, high enough to tower over the prairieland, Cade's mountain loomed in ghostly illumination, as distant, as eerie, and as lonely, as God.

He walked at her side to the front pathway, saw the lights inside where her father was, and stooped to kiss her tenderly. Then he said, 'Do you still want to go to the uplands with me?'

She leaned her cheek against his chest. 'Tonight?'

'No. First we got to see Preacher Given. After that.'

She snuggled closer, running both strong arms round him. 'When will we go see the preacher?'

'. . . How about right after breakfast tomorrow morning?'

She moved her head up and down against him. Then she suddenly pushed back, kissed him recklessly on the lips and whirled to rush into the house. It all happened very fast.

He thought he understood. He had glimpsed the tears and the tight-held mouth. He knew for a fact that female-things registered a lot of things, all the way from fury to love, from poignancy to passion, with tears.

Still; it left him shaken. On the slow way home he also thought he had been reckless. Before they did any-thing, he should speak to her father. And after that, the preacher. Old Cade sure had been right about life being a trail without end. A man thought he knew a lot, then he got up the very next morning and learned something new all over again.

TWENTY

THE OTHER PLACE

They went high to the hills leaving Alex Far-raday, Reverend Given, and two others, Dick Ullman and Stuart Campbell, standing back in hard silence, watching them out of sight.

They were each of them a little breathless, a little uncertain. It took getting accustomed to this business of being lovers, and at the same time husband and wife. Old Stuart had taken Douglas aside to be severe with him.

'Dang it, boy, girls don't just want to be fetched up

short and hitched, like a damned work-horse. They want family and friends and flowers, and all that sort of thing.'

Douglas had agreed. Then he had pointed to where Angeline and her father had been talking to Reverend Given. 'Go tell her that.'

Old Campbell had looked over where Angeline had been, but he had not moved an inch. 'You mean to say she *don't?*'

'She told me this morning she wanted it just like this. You and her paw, and a few others, as few as possible, then get on our way.'

Old Campbell had wagged his head. He had not objected to being Best Man, although he'd scarcely had time to shed his work-apron and recover from the astonishment before Dick and Alex had hustled him across to the parson's parlour, and if he'd had all day to get ready he couldn't have shown up looking much different anyway, because he did not own a suit.

As they were mounting up Ullman had walked over looking uncomfortable. He was a man with a long memory, evidently, because as he offered a big paw to Douglas, he had said, 'Son, when you folks get back, put up your horses in my barn. Mind now; I don't want to hear they been put up somewhere else.'

It was hard not to like a man, even a man like Dick Ullman, on some days, while on other days it was easy to dislike him. As Douglas rode along towards the distant pass leading to the topout at Cade's mountain, he told this to Angeline.

Her reply did not seem to have anything at all to do with his remark. She looked tenderly over and said, 'I want to cry when I think of your mother, Douglas. She'd be so proud of you.'

They had the flatland at their back and the mountains dead ahead all morning and most of the afternoon. The sun was like an immense egg-yolk by the time he led Angeline into the brakes and out the far side where the old trail began. They had made good time. He particularly wanted to make good time, even though he was thoughtful of her. But she seemed to be equally as urgent, or perhaps it was that she sensed his urgency. In either case when he asked, many times on the trail, if she wanted to stop for a while, she smiled and shook her head.

He thought she was tougher than she looked. He already knew she was stronger. What he did *not* know of course, was that toughness had nothing to do with it as far as she was concerned. She was a wife, a married woman; she belonged to the lean, wide-shouldered handsome man up ahead. If he kept riding all day and all night and all the next day and next night, she would follow. Physical convenience or inconvenience would not enter into it.

The sun hung poised, more egg-yolk-like than ever, upon a high peak far beyond Cade's mountain, then it broke and red-orange late-day light flooded downwards in the sun's final flash of glory, carrying quick, hard brilliance downward and outward—but only briefly—then the glare passed and the brilliance followed, until just the hour-long soft afterglow remained. They rode on up the Cade-mountain trail through that hour, and the previous as well as the ensuing hour.

It was forest from the foothills, but a thicker and darker and vaster forest, after they left the first lift and reached the next rise. Here, there was a hurrying creek. Beyond, another hour, with sunset lingering even though its source, the sun, was gone, they passed through a park where columbine in violet and yellow, in white and red, grew on delicate stalks. After that the shadows came down from each treetop with a soft and clinging gloom, and when Angeline looked up, she was dwarfed by trees, by oncoming darkness, by the vastness, by the far-away great peaks, and by the kind of silence she had never encountered before. She urged her horse to stay up closer.

They talked very little after the darkness arrived, but Angeline was confident. Anxious, and slightly afraid, but confident, because Douglas slouched along up ahead as though he knew every twist and turn—which he did—in the vague trail they followed. She admired the breadth of his back, the night-hung outline of his shoulders, the lankiness and the ease of him.

At times he reminded her of a little boy. At other times he was as profound and thoughtful and quiet as a much older man. She thought that he had missed a lot, not growing up with other little boys, but she also thought that, as unconventional as his upbringing had been, it was better. For him; perhaps not for all boys, but for him it had been exactly right. But Douglas Weldon was a strong man. If he had not been, if Old Cade had found himself saddled with a whining weakling . . . She had to stop there. She had seen Old Cade and she had heard from her father among others, about him, but she really had not known him, actually, so she could not finish her thought.

She did not have to anyway.

It was cooler up on Cade's mountain than it had been back in North Fork. When Douglas halted and offered her his coat she had declined. He then led off again, saying it was not much farther.

It turned out not to be, unless two additional miles on a saddle were a great distance to someone who had ridden more this day than she had ever ridden in one time before, in her whole lifetime.

Then they were on the lip of mountain plateau with starshine outlining the old cabin, and far below and far out, the ghostly prairieland, and nearer, in the still and endless backgrounding distance, the face of the forest with its fragrance and its endlessness.

Douglas stepped down and went back to raise both arms to her. She eased forward and let him hold her after she touched the ground. She twisted to look again, from within his arms. North Fork was invisible, but it was down there. He pointed and told her that was where the town stood, but there was no way to tell.

They put up the horses first, threw them hay and made certain the corrals were barred down where Old Cade had made an opening for creek-water to flow through one end. Afterwards, he took her by the hand out to the edge of the bluff and while she felt tiny and insignificant before the enormity and sweep of the view, he said, 'You are now on Cade's mountain.' He grinned. 'You'll probably be eating standing up for the next few days, but I didn't want to stop until we got here.'

She was glad, now, that he hadn't wanted to stop. He took her around back and showed her the little stone hut where the traps were kept, showed her their smoke-house. He and Old Cade had built that, had shredded the tree-bark to stuff between the two walls, inner wall and outer wall. He showed her the circular drying frames for beaver pelts, and took her by one hand out through a dark stand of huge trees to a stumped-off clearing. There, it was possible just by looking up, to see the eternally snow-necklaced highest peak. By starlight and weak moonshine, the peak looked like it plunged straight through the heavens into the Beyond.

She nestled against him. 'It has to have a name, Douglas.'

It did have. He gave it to her in Dahkota, then repeated it in English, but it lost too much that way, so he tried to explain. 'It's called Big Face. Well; that's how it comes out in our language. But what is meant is that it's *the* face of *the* god. God's face, I reckon, is how I ought to say it. But it doesn't come out the same in English.' He turned her back towards the cabin. 'We've got a week or a month, or as long as you can stand it, before we have to go back down there, so why not take our time?'

He took her into the old cabin, which was large and long and fort-like in its indestructible strength, but it was also a place where only a man and a boy had lived. It lacked everything a woman's touch would have lent it.

It was not cold, although it would be later, but Douglas rustled kindling from a box in the wall, and built a fire anyway. The fireplace had been Old Cade's pride. There were no big rocks near the place where the cabin stood. Old Cade had carried those boulders on a horse-drawn travois for a full year, off and on, before he'd had enough to build his fireplace and chimney.

It was a warm, snug place, with sturdy furniture fashioned on bitter winter days and through many a very long winter night, by a man whose ingenuity and pride in craftsmanship were evident in everything he built.

The kitchen had an iron stove, carried up there part by part many years before. Douglas took Angeline through the rooms. He showed her where he had stayed as a child, and the larger, better room he and Old Cade had built on, one summer, after he was in his teens.

They ended up out back, in the kitchen, where Douglas surprised her by being an adept cook. He could make a meal that was varied and hot and filling. He even made her a cup of chocolate. Old Cade had always considered things like tinned chocolate almost shameful luxuries. It had to be a particularly momentous event for him to break out the tin. Like the first bear Douglas shot, and the biggest trout he caught in a lake beyond the outback clearing. On Christmas Eve and on their birthdays, although neither one of them had been very certain which day actually was their birthday, so they worked it out as close as they thought it had to be one winter night, and always afterwards that had been it, for them both.

Angeline sat and listened, and watched him work at the stove, at their supper table with a coal-oil lamp hanging overhead, and loved him, and wanted to laugh at him sometime, and felt an ache in her heart too.

They finished eating long before they left the kitchen. It was so quiet; so easy to be there without any sensation of time passing at all. She felt as though nothing had ever happened before, as though she had never *seen* things or felt them as deeply as she felt them on Cade's mountain.

The fire was burning and as she sank down upon the great couch and watched him put the lamp upon the mantle, she had the distinct sensation of being older, or having been here with him for a very long while, and when he came back to drop down beside her and watch the fire twist and curl she said, 'It isn't the same up here as it was down there, is it?'

He looked at her and smiled. 'No. I don't reckon it ever will be, either. Never again. Not for me, anyway. But maybe not in the same way as you're thinking. I've never seen a woman here before, and now, whatever happens, I'll never come here again without seeing *two* of you. Old Cade and you.'

It was very pleasant in the warmth and in the drowsy light. Outside, an owl called, and from farther off another owl answered. He had heard this so many previous times up here that he hardly heeded it, except that tonight the sound was not as sad as it usually seemed.

She lay her head upon his shoulder and said, 'I'll tell you a secret, if you'd like me to. My grandmother used to tell my father stories about Old Cade.' She raised her face to him. 'My grandmother was a Sioux.'

He was not really surprised. He had never put his mind to it, but somewhere, in the back of his mind, there was some kind of inherent knowledge about this. It was in her father's eyes and it was also in her eyes, as black as midnight, as deep and depthless as Time itself. It was also in her midnight hair and her golden skin, and in the tall, proud way she moved and walked and carried herself.

She kept looking at him. 'You're not surprised?'

He said, 'I reckon not. I think I knew it all along.'

'Does it make any difference to you?'

He laughed and slid an arm around her. 'Sure. It

means that now I understand why you've got strength and toughness. And you're the prettiest thing I've ever seen. But maybe that doesn't have much to do with it. You'd be beautiful no matter what.'

Her head dropped back to his shoulder. 'When I first saw you ride into town, Douglas, from the store-window, you were leading your horse up the road from the direction of Ullman's barn. You were carrying that old rifle in one arm . . . Do you know what I thought?'

'No.'

'That my grandmother would have wanted to know you—if she'd still been alive.'

He lifted her chin with a bent finger and brushed her lips with his mouth. 'Too bad she isn't. Too bad Old Cade isn't too.' She raised up and twisted against him, both arms reaching.

'Maybe they are, Douglas. Maybe they know. Maybe it's just *us* that aren't supposed to know.' She pulled him down. 'Cade was right; people have to share thoughts as well as needs.' She pressed her flushed cheek to his face. 'I always thought love was something that—well—just came sort of gradually, and a girl married a man, and they had a family, and it was all orderly.'

He said, 'It isn't though.'

She twisted harder against him. 'It can't be. Not with us. I don't know how we could have managed it, back down there, with people everywhere.'

He folded both arms around her. There would be no

people up here, no boys with tridents going frogging to interrupt. For as long as they wished, they would be alone together on Cade's mountain.

The owls were silent, the fire crackled and burnt low, the bands of time that overlapped and went in a great circle continued to turn and turn, and for Douglas Cade Weldon the trail without end had reached a new height, a fresh plateau.

Center Point Publishing
600 Brooks Road • PO Box 1
Thorndike ME 04986-0001 USA

(207) 568-3717

US & Canada:
1 800 929-9108